Roger Hall

G.T.M.

Desperately, Shaun dragged Catsfoot towards the window.

(See Cha[

GUN TOWN MARSHAL

A 'Catsfoot' Western

by
JOHN ROBB

Dear Boys,

You probably know that Catsfoot and his guns made a brief but very dramatic appearance in one of my "Captain Shelby" Westerns.

Soon after that book came out I received letters asking for more about Catsfoot. They pleased me very much, because it happened that I was already writing *Gun Town Marshal*.

Well, here it is, the first story featuring that legendary trail scout. Let me know whether you like it—I enjoy answering your letters.

With best wishes,

JOHN ROBB.

CONTENTS

CHAPTER ONE

"I'LL KEEP THE PEACE"

SHAUN'S father unhooked his gun belt from the wall and buckled it round his waist. Then he knotted the leg-cord. Shaun watched, feeling a flicker of fear. He chanced a question.

"What's the matter, pop?"

Herb Brent, marshal of Gloryrise, gave his son a strained smile.

"There could be trouble comin'," he said. "Whatever happens, you've gotta stay right here in my office."

"What sort of trouble, pop?"

"The Guthrie outfit are headed this way. They'll be here in just a few minutes."

Shaun's tongue became suddenly dry, his throat tight. He said shakily: "Guthrie...! I didn't think they'd bother about us!"

"Neither did I, Shaun. But it looks like they'll try to take over this town for lootin' and killin', like they've done in a whole lotta other places in the territory."

Brent drew his .38 Colt "Bulldog" as he finished speaking. He flipped open the loading gate. There was a soft whirring sound as he spun

the cylinder, checking the six centre-fire cart-
ridges. Satisfied, he dropped the short-barrel
gun back in its holster. Then his stocky figure
moved towards the door. But Shaun—who at
fourteen was as tall as his father—blocked the
way.

"Pop!"

"Well, son?"

"You're … you're not goin' to try to shoot it
out with Guthrie!"

Brent put a hand on Shaun's shoulder.

"I hope there won't be any shootin', son. I'm
the marshal here and my job's to keep the peace,
so I'm goin' to try to persuade Guthrie and his
outfit to keep ridin' right out of our town."

"But if they won't?"

"Then mebbe I'll *have* to shoot."

Shaun said urgently: "You can't talk like that!
Guthrie's the fastest gun in the territory!"

"So they say … but I'm fast, too."

"So you are, but you're nowhere near Guthrie's
class, pop!" Shaun was breathing quickly. Sweat
was on his face as he added: "Guthrie's a professional gun-slinger and a killer. He'd get you!"

Brent shrugged. Then he touched the silver
star on his left breast.

"I was elected marshal to protect the folks of
Gloryrise," he said, "and protect 'em I will. I
ain't no hero, but I ain't yellow, neither. That
means I'll do m'duty."

"Okay, pop, but don't let 'em goad you into any gunplay! Even if Guthrie didn't fix you, one of the others would. I've heard there's more than twenty men in that outfit, so you wouldn't have a chance!"

Brent was a stubborn man. When he set a course he did not waver from it. He said flatly: "I can look after myself. You don't have to worry about me, son."

But Shaun was far from convinced.

Like everyone in Arizona, he had been told plenty about Guthrie and his outfit.

He had been told how they moved into the smaller towns like victorious vandals, terrorising the people and seizing whatever they wanted.

Shaun had been told that sometimes men dared to defend their property. Or a law officer had the courage to do his duty. They never survived....

Each of that outfit was a top-gun. Each a killer.

And the fastest, the most dangerous of them all was Guthrie. Shaun had often heard it said that no man breathed who could equal Guthrie's speed to the draw. Men whispered: "There's somethin' unreal about the way he pulls a gun... it happens so fast, you don't see nothin'!"

Guthrie's outfit was the most feared of the outlaw bands, although there were many others. For in this year of 1868 Arizona was in semi-chaos. The recent Civil War was the reason. While the war was being fought, all troops had been withdrawn from the territory. Now, after the Federal victory, the soldiers were returning— but only to find that in many areas the Apaches were in revolt. Thinly scattered military posts, desperately trying to control the Apaches, could not also spare men to deal with white renegades. And they never had any reason to go near Gloryrise. For the people of Gloryrise were lucky to be on fairly friendly terms with the nearby redskin encampment. In fact, a small amount of barter trade went on between the Indians and the towns- folk.

Those thoughts flitted through Shaun's mind as he stood opposite his father. Then he heard a heavy tread on the board-walk outside. The town's two deputies strode into the office. They were hard men, those deputies. Hard like hickory.

One of them, a corn-cob pipe in his bearded face, was carrying a Sharp's single-shot rifle. Shaun knew it was a useful weapon, but out- dated. It was slow to load, needing a separate percussion cap behind the linen cartridge.

The other deputy, who was the younger and taller of the two, had a .44 "First Dragoon" in his holster. That was a popular six-shot re- volver and one of the Colt firm's first models.

Both those men were tense. They licked their lips as they looked at Brent.

The younger of them said: "We're ready, Marshal."

"I'm glad to know it. You've warned the folks to keep off the street?"

"Yep, they're all under cover."

The bearded deputy patted the stock of his rifle. He said: "We could use some help, Marshal. Why don't you let a few of the men in this burgh stand with us? You could swear 'em in as extra deputies."

But Brent shook his head.

"If we make a big show of force, we'd be sure to spark off trouble," he said, "then the whole durned town'd be shot up and mebbe innocent people would be killed. That's just what I don't want, so we'll try to handle this ourselves— quietly. I figure it's our only chance."

The bearded deputy looked doubtful. But he said: "Okay, you're boss here... but I sure hope Guthrie decides not to linger in Gloryrise."

The deputies turned and moved out, Brent following them. Shaun put out a hand towards his father as he passed. Brent paused for a moment and their eyes met. Shaun saw fear in his father's face. He had never seen it there before. But something else was there, too. It was the will to overcome that fear. The two added up to simple, raw courage.

"Pop... good luck."

Shaun had wanted to say more, but could not. Brent touched his land. Then he was gone, with the others.

And Shaun was alone in the law office. Alone in the small, spruce-wood room with its teak desk, a couple of chairs, an iron box containing official papers, a picture of Abraham Lincoln, and a pendulum clock ticking in a corner. That clock showed seven minutes after five.

Shaun went to the window.

It was as if Gloryrise had died. Had, in an evil stroke, suddenly become a ghost town. Usually at this time, when the worst of the day's heat was done, the town was bustling with plainsmen, copper miners, gossiping women and scampering children. But not now.

Now all doors were closed, probably barred. Many of the windows were shuttered. The main street was deserted—save for his father and the two deputies, who were talking in the centre of the rutted road, opposite the office. But it was only a short conversation. It ended with all of them nodding. Then Brent remained where he was while the deputies spread out to the boardwalks on each side of him.

The bearded deputy leaned against a hitching-rail. He was within a couple of yards of Shaun's window. He noticed Shaun and his words came faintly through the glass as he said: "You'd better stand back, kid. It ain't so safe, there."

Shaun tried to look as if he had not understood the warning.

The deputy repeated: "It ain't safe…"

That was as far as he got.

He broke off, suddenly tensing like a compressed spring and staring towards the south end of the street. The two others were staring in the same direction. They had heard something.

Then Shaun heard it, too. Distant, but approaching fast. The thudding of many hoofs.

There was menace in that sound. Like the gathering of dry thunder before a storm. Some stray dog, scared by it, gave a long and mournful howl.

Shaun pressed his face against the glass. There was a slight bend at the end of the street, which would make it impossible to see the horsemen until they were actually in Gloryrise. But there would not be long to wait.

A swirl of dust rose from beyond the most distant framewood buildings. The beat of hoofs was racing to a crescendo.

Then, in columns of two, the Guthrie outfit rode into the town.

They were moving at a fast trot and when they first appeared they were about two hundred yards away. Gradually they slackened pace. They reined in when their front files were less than a dozen paces from Brent and his deputies.

As he looked at them, Shaun felt a renewed sensation of helplessness. Their looks more than confirmed the worst stories about them….

Some were swart and arrogant Mexicans, who recognised only the law of the gun.

Others had begun their lives as killers in California, in the desert planes of Utah, in the newly-discovered gold-mining territory of Colorado.

A few of them were half-breed Indians, vicious of temper and quick to throw a knife.

Nearly all of them carried ammunition bandoliers over their shoulders and modern repeating rifles in their saddle clasps.

They were a cross-section of the scum of a continent. Even as they sat on their sweating horses, relaxed and caked with trail dirt, they exuded undiluted evil. It was something which could be felt as well as seen.

But none showed it more than the man who was at the head of them.

Guthrie....

He was big, this Guthrie. Big as a bull is big. Massively ugly, glaringly dangerous. His face was square and unshaven. The eyes were dark holes within it, unblinking like those of an animal. A black fedora was pushed far back on his crinkled jet hair. The front of his filthy blue shirt was open, showing huge chest muscles.

Shaun's eyes travelled to Guthrie's gun.

There was no escaping that gun. He wore it so that it must be seen, must be respected. Even at rest, it was a warning. The belt and holster were polished so that they glittered red-brown. The butt of his .44 Colt "Frontier" was edged with silver. It was obviously a superb weapon, probably designed to a special specification. He was carrying it well forward, partly resting against the front of his right leg, so as to use the cross-wise sweeping draw which was preferred by many gunslingers.

Guthrie from his saddle looked down on Herb Brent. And Brent, completely still, stared back at him. There was a clink of bridle chains. A snort from one horse, an impatient stamp from another. Those were the only sounds for several agonised seconds.

It was Guthrie who spoke first. His voice had a brittle rasp which was near to a shout.

"You the marshal of this burgh?"

Brent looked slowly down at his badge. Then back again at Guthrie. He said quietly: "You can see that. I guess you're Guthrie?"

Guthrie smiled. It was humourless, unlovely.

"It's nice to be known," he said. "Makes me feel kind of welcome."

"You ain't welcome here. Anyway, this is a law-abidin' town and it ain't a rich one, so you won't find anythin' to keep you in it."

Guthrie looked carefully around him, twisting in his saddle. He said: "You're too modest, Marshal. I figure me and m'outfit can use this burgh for a few days."

Brent shook his head.

"I don't see it that way. I'm askin' you to move on, Guthrie, 'cause we don't want trouble."

"Why talk about trouble? There'll be none of that—just so long as the folks here are nice and hospitable."

"Yep, I know what that means," Brent said, his voice suddenly rising. "It means everything'll be okay if you're allowed to loot the town. Well, it ain't goin' to happen in Gloryrise!"

Guthrie leaned forward on his saddle pommel.

"You're talkin' mighty big, Marshal! D'you figure that you and a couple of deputies can do anything? Mebbe you're forgettin', but I've got more than twenty men at the back of me."

"And I've got the law behind me!"

"You're wrong there, Marshal. Wherever I go, *I'm* the law!"

Brent wiped his wet forehead with the back of a hand. That hand was shaking. But he wasn't retreating an inch.

"You must feel good and brave with a small army to shoot for you," he said. "But you don't scare me none."

Guthrie's animal eyes became slits, his voice a bellow.

"I don't need anyone to shoot for me, Marshal! I carry the fastest gun on earth!"

"Mebbe you do, but we don't need any fast guns around these parts, so get..."

Guthrie interrupted. He said less loudly: "I'll make a deal with you."

"I don't deals with folks like you."

"Mebbe you'll be interested in this one, Marshal."

"Okay—what is it?"

Guthrie paused. The humourless smile deepened. He said: "My outfit will pass right through this town without hurtin' no one, provided you do me one little favour."

Brent was watching him cautiously. He asked: "And what kinda favour would that be?"

"Just reach for your gun!"

"Y'mean I've got to..."

"You've got to try to take me in a gunfight, Marshal. If you do that, my outfit'll quit this place right away, that's my pledge."

"If I fail? If you nail me?"

Guthrie gave a short laugh. It seemed to gather in the depth of his stomach.

"Then you won't be around to worry about what happens to Gloryrise," he said. "But it's your only chance, Marshal. If you *don't* draw on me, we'll take the town apart anyway."

Shaun moved....

He was not aware of making any decision to rush out of that office. It just happened. It happened instinctively. Suddenly he was on the board-walk, vaulting over the hitching-rail, pushing past the bearded deputy. He ran towards his father and grasped his gun arm.

"Don't do it, Pop! Don't try to out-draw Guthrie!"

Brent looked steadily at his son. At the same time he pulled his arm free.

"I told you to keep out of this, Shaun," he said. "You ain't a man yet and this ain't none of your business."

"But it is... he'll be sure to kill you!"

"It's my one chance to save the folks of Gloryrise and I'm takin' it."

"Pop... it isn't a chance! It's just plain murder!"

As he spoke, Shaun tried to renew the grip on his father's gun arm. But Brent backed away.

Then Guthrie spoke. His booming tones came like a barrier between them and both froze still.

"Mebbe the kid's right," Guthrie was saying. "Mebbe a straight gunfight wouldn't give the marshal a clean deal."

He had dismounted. He was standing legs apart, hands on his thick thighs.

"I've a different idea," Guthrie continued. "I'm goin' to make it easy for the marshal. Look..."

Slowly he lifted his hands until they were above his head.

Brent was obviously puzzled. He asked: "Why're you doin' that, Guthrie?"

"Because I'm givin' you a big opportunity, Marshal."

"Thanks—but I still don't get it."

"It's simple, Marshal. Y'see, I'll keep my hands up here, but you can keep yours at your side. Then, when someone gives the word, we'll both go for our guns. That ought to even it up. I figure I'm bein' kind of generous."

It was a piece of extraordinary bravado. Guthrie seemed to be placing himself at an impossible disadvantage, for his gun hand would have to travel fully three feet to the holster while Brent's moved only a few inches. But shaun did not feel any less anxious. Shaun knew that ordinary notions of what was possible just did not apply to professional gunfighters such as Guthrie.

It was not just a freak of nature which made those gunfighters fantastically fast—although natural flair came into it. To acquire their speed they made a careful—almost scientific—study of arm and wrist movements, just as a wrestler studies locks and throws. And they practised. It was said that a man must work at drawing and shooting for at least three hours a day for five years before he could hope to attain the skill of a recognised top-gun. But that was not all. Afterwards, about two hours daily had to be spent on more training, to keep the muscles supple and the reflexes sharp.

To become a genuine top-gun called for sacrifice and rigid self-discipline. The result could be a speed and accuracy which seemed to defy the laws of nature.

There were certainly not more than a few hundred top-guns in the entire vast western territories, although many thousands who were just ordinarily fast claimed the title.

And of the top-guns, Guthrie was believed to be supreme. So was he taking any real risk against Brent? Shaun asked himself the question. The answer was clear enough—Guthrie still held a huge advantage, even though Brent was no fool with a Colt.

Brent, too, must have known that, for he seemed to waver uncertainly.

Guthrie said: "It seems like you're real yellow, Marshal! Ain't you goin' to draw on me?"

Brent muttered: "I ain't yellow. I'll draw."

"That's fine," Guthrie said. Then he glanced at Shaun and added: "The kid can give the word. Go on, kid! Shout up nice and loud and see what your pop can do!"

Shaun felt as if he were being held in a steel-jawed trap. He dreaded to give that signal to draw. But there was no way out. He dragged in a breath. He tried to utter the word. But nothing emerged. Nothing save the faintest croak, which he alone could hear.

Brent said: "Do like he says, Shaun. I'm ready."

Shaun tried again.

This time he must have called out clearly. He must have shouted *"Draw...!"* Yet he did not catch the sound of his own voice.

Too much happened too quickly.

Too much which was sickeningly evil.

Guthrie's right hand was above his head. Then it vanished. It was made invisible by sheer speed. In the same moment there was a blurred impression of a gun. Guthrie's gun. It seemed to leap into the air in a glitter of silver.

There was a purple flash, made faint by the sun.

And a crash which reverberated through Glory-rise.

Plus a wisp of smoke which carried the sulphurous smell of burnt powder.

Brent....?

His Colt "Bulldog" was in his hand. But he had not squeezed the trigger. It was waving wildly and he was spinning on one leg like a top. Suddenly he ceased to spin and he gave a long groan. He dropped his gun and pressed his left hand against his right shoulder. Blood trickled between the fingers.

Guthrie laughed again. And now he was crouching—his whole powerful body bent forward like a bear about to drop on easy prey.

"That's just winged you, Marshal! But you're alive! Ain't you grateful to me for lettin' you live?"

The skin of Brent's face was drawn tight against the bones. His voice was shaking as he said: "I'm surprised, Guthrie... . I thought you shot to kill."

"I do ... and I'm goin' to kill you right now, Marshal. I just wanted to shake you up first...."

He thumbed back his gun hammer. Carefully, deliberately taking plenty of time, he aimed at the centre of Brent's chest. He took first pressure on the trigger, his finger moving only a fraction.

Then he fired.

But he did not fire at Brent.

Guthrie flicked his wrist to the right. For a hideous second Shaun thought that the bullet was intended for him. He felt a breath of displaced air as the hot slug passed within inches of his head. Then Shaun heard a brief gasping sound behind him, mingling with the echoing explosion.

It came from the bearded deputy. He was falling forward. Going down like a toppled sack. He lay utterly still when he hit the ground, his Sharp's rifle under his stomach.

Guthrie said: "He was goin' to try to nick me. He had ideas about shootin' from waist level, but it ain't got him any place, 'cause I was watchin' him, too." Guthrie paused. He looked towards the other deputy, who was standing at the opposite side of the street. This was Matthew, the younger man. His legs were braced against the board-walk and he was rigid with hopeless fear. The courage had drained out of him as water drains through sand. He could not be blamed. Matthew was normally brave enough. But all men have their limit, and he had reached his.

Guthrie boomed at him: "D'you want to play the hero, too? Are you thinkin' of aimin' a sly slug at me?"

The remaining deputy, eyes wide, shook his head.

"I ain't aimin' to get m'self killed for nothin'," he said. "I only..."

The words faded out, lost in a burst of shouting. It was Brent.

Brent, with one good arm, had thrown himself at Guthrie. And Guthrie, who must have written off any chance of danger from the wounded marshal, was taken entirely by surprise. Brent crashed against him in a long leap. The two swayed and went down together, Brent on top. His left hand was clawing for a hold round Guthrie's neck. He almost got one. His fingers made a half-circle and his thumb began to press against the windpipe. Then Guthrie jerked up both knees. Brent was lifted into the air. He landed partly on his back, partly on the left side of his head. It was the head blow which did it—it knocked Brent senseless. He twitched, then lay as if asleep.

Some of the horsemen had dismounted. They rushed towards Brent and stood hesitantly over the unconscious figure, their guns out. Shaun pushed through them and kneeled beside his father. He was breathing regularly enough, but a glance showed that he must be getting very weak, for the shoulder wound was bleeding freely. And it would not stop until the slug was removed.

Shaun heard one of the men say to Guthrie: "It looks like the marshal's still got big ideas. Shall I finish him?"

"Nope ... there ain't any satisfaction in killin' a man when he doesn't know anythin' about it. He won't give us any more trouble by the looks of him. I guess we'll start makin' ourselves comfortable in this town...."

They moved away.

Some leading their horses, some riding them, they went towards the only hotel in Gloryrise, which was at the far end of the street.

And shaun was alone with his unconscious father.

Alone except for Matthew, the younger deputy, who shuffled nervously towards him. They did not speak, but each knew what to do. The deputy lifted Brent's shoulders while Shaun took the legs. They carried him into the office, then into a room at the back, where he had a trestle bunk. They laid him on it, covered him with a blanket.

Shaun said: "I'm gettin' the doctor—you put a pad over that wound."

But the deputy was already doing that. Without looking up, he said: "I...I guess I wasn't much use to your pop, Shaun, I'm sorry... I was so scared I just seized up."

"It ain't your fault," Shaun told him. "Anyone would have cracked out there."

Then he ran out of the building.

Gloryrise was stirring again. But slowly, reluctantly, like a person afraid to open his eyes for fear of what they might see. Window shutters were being cautiously raised and strained faces peered through them. A few doors were unbolted and men stood sheepishly in the thresholds. A very small child scampered into the middle of the street. Its mother gave a warning shriek before darting out and carrying it back.

Guthrie's outfit were no longer in sight. Their horses were hitched outside the hotel. They would be inside it, taking over the rooms, terrorising the owner.

Shaun turned towards the house where the town doctor lived. But the doctor was already approaching, running towards the marshal's office, anxious to get under cover again as soon as possible.

He blinked at Shaun through wire-rimmed spectacles and asked breathlessly: "Is your father still alive?"

Shaun nodded and led the way back to the bunk where Brent lay. There the doctor felt his pulse, then cut away the clothing over the wounded shoulder. He probed the raw cavity with a steel instrument.

"The slug's in deep," the doctor said to Shaun and the deputy. "You two'll have to help me get it out...."

It was almost dark and they had lit the kerosene lamp above Brent's bed. His chest was white with bandages, his face a grey-yellow. But he was conscious and the doctor was saying to him: "You'll be okay, Marshal, but you'll have to lie up for a few weeks. You'll need proper nursing and I'm fixing for a couple of women to look after you."

Brent murmured: "What's happenin' in the town? What... what's Guthrie doin'?"

"It's all quiet right now," the doctor said. "You don't have to worry. I'm leaving you now, but I'll be in again soon."

He straightened his spectacles, made a last check of the bandages, then picked up his bag and went out. The deputy followed.

Shaun sat on the edge of the trestle bed. Brent gave him a weak smile.

"You were right, Shaun... I never had a chance against Guthrie."

"Nobody would have a chance against him, Pop. The way he draws a gun just ain't human."

Brent hesitated. Then he said: "I'm goin' to tell you somethin' mighty important, son.

You've got to listen carefully and you've got to believe me."

"Of course I'll believe you, Pop. What is it?"

"You remember I once told you about a trail scout I used to know called Catsfoot."

Puzzled, Shaun nodded and said: "Yep, I remember. You said he was one of the best scouts there is and a fine man, too."

"That's right, but there's somethin' I never mentioned 'cause this Catsfoot don't like people to know about it. You see ... he's a top-gun. A *real* top-gun. And he's faster than Guthrie! I've seen them both now, and I just *know* Catsfoot's faster than Guthrie! He carries two guns ... slung kind of low. Years back, I saw him draw them in Tucson City, when a half-breed tried to throw a knife into a man's back. I tell you, Catsfoot drew his guns and blew that blade to pieces when it was spinnin' through the air! Yep, he did that and I ain't talkin' crazy!"

There was a frantic urgency about Brent which could not be ignored. Despite all else, Shaun was fascinated. He knew that there were two types of gun-slingers. The majority of them were outlaws who wanted people to know of their skill so as to spread terror and make their work easier. The others were law-abiding men. Their skill was acquired and used only for self-defence, or for the defence of others. And they usually preferred to keep quiet about their speed, so as not to attract

unnecessary trouble. Therefore it was quite possible that this trail scout was a genuine top-gun.
But faster than Guthrie? Shaun could not bring
himself to believe that.

Shaun asked: "Why are you tellin' me this,
Pop?"

"'Cause right now, Catsfoot's only five miles
from here! He's livin' in that cabin at Oxby
Tops!"

Shaun remembered the cabin. It was on the
bank of a dried-up river. It had once been
used by a gold-panner, but had long since been
deserted.

"But what's he doin' there, Pop? There ain't
nothin' for a trail scout in that place."

"I've been wonderin' the same, Shaun. It
seems like there's a bit of mystery about it, but it
ain't any of our business. All I know for sure is
that he settled in there a couple of days ago. I
was goin' to ride out to pay him a friendly call, but
I can't do that now … not me."

Shaun understood. He asked: "Shall I go
out to see him?"

"That's what I want you to do."

"And ask him to ride into town?"

"Just tell him what's happenin' here, then I
figure Catsfoot will be with us quick enough."

Shaun got off the edge of the bed and paced the
tiny room. He felt a sudden surge of hope. But it
vanished as he considered the facts. He said:

"But pop, what good would it do if Catsfoot does come into town? He's only one man! Guthrie has more than twenty."

Slowly Brent turned his head to look up at Shaun. He asked: "Why d'you think I tried to fight it out with Guthrie?"

"Why" Well ... cause you're the marshal."

"Yep, but that's not all. First, I was hopin' Guthrie's outfit would leave us alone, and that's why I didn't ask any of the other townsfolk to stand with us. I just didn't want to provoke trouble. But when...when I saw there could be no peace I decided to face up to Guthrie. I guess I knew I never had a chance, but I wanted to set an example. That way, I figured I might give a bit of courage to the town, so they'd fight instead of waitin' to be knocked on the head like rabbits. Y'see, son, if ordinary folks in towns like this all stood together, even Guthrie's mob wouldn't have a chance."

Shaun said softly: "You were durned nearly killed, Pop. And no one followed you, except one deputy. They were just too scared."

"Mebbe that's right, Shaun, but I don't blame them. In a way it was my fault, 'cause I'm not a natural leader. There *are* men that ordinary folks will follow through any danger. Those men ... mebbe they don't talk so much, but they can set a flame alight in the hearts of people when it comes to fightin' for things that are good and decent.

I'm not one like that, but Catsfoot is ... I know it. When Catsfoot comes into town, he won't be alone for long. Soon he'll have everyone behind him and the Guthrie outfit'll have to quit. That's why I want you to tell him what's goin' on here."

"I understand now, Pop. I'll saddle your horse and leave right away. But say...this Catsfoot sure sounds like some man!"

"He ain't like the sort of men we see every day, Shaun. There's a kind of magic about him. Mebbe that sounds just durned silly, but you'll know what I mean just as soon as you meet him."

Shaun could not resist one more question, although his father was obviously tired and in pain.

"Catsfoot's a strange name. Is it his real one?

"I guess it's not, son, but everyone calls him that. It's on account of the way he walks. He's silent ... just like a cat, I guess. Now you go find him."

There was a movement in the doorway. Then a laugh; that deep and humourless laugh.

Shaun spun round. Guthrie was there. He was leaning against the doorpost, thumbs thrust under his gunbelt.

"No need to put the kid to a lot of trouble," he said.

Brent tried to raise himself from the pillow, but

fell back groaning. He said in a hard whisper: "What d'you mean, Guthrie?"

"I mean *I'll* ride to Oxby Tops right now... me and a few of m'outfit. This Catsfoot hombre you've been talkin' about won't be expectin' us, so we ought to be able to fix him easy."

CHAPTER TWO

THE CABIN

Fix him easy...!

THE words bit into Shaun's brain like drops of acid. They could mean only one thing—that Catsfoot would be taken by surprise. The rest would be simple murder. Outnumbered, he would be helpless, even though he was a top-gun. Guthrie and his men would never give him a chance.

Unless he could be warned.

In that moment, Shaun knew that somehow he must get to that cabin. And get there ahead of Guthrie. But how? His father's horse was in the stable at the back of the building. He could not go there without Guthrie seeing him. And it would take two or three minutes to saddle the animal.

Guthrie was coming into the room. Ambling towards the bed, the better to exult over Brent.

Shaun glanced through the half-open door into the office. No lamp had been lit in there, but the light from the room showed that the place was empty. The outer door was ajar, too, and there was no sign of anyone. It seemed that Guthrie was alone.

And Guthrie, now standing over that bunk, had his back to him.

Very slowly, absolutely silently, Shaun moved towards the adjacent office. He made a calculation. He decided that, once in the comparative gloom, he might be able to slip through the outer door, then dart round to the back and saddle the horse. With a lot of luck he could manage it and get a short start.

He moved sideways, eyes on Guthrie. His steps were short and agonised. He took three of them. He was partly in the office. Sweating and trying to control his breathing, he braced himself for a dash which would take him outside the building. One foot was raised.

Then Guthrie spoke.

"Where d'you think you're goin', kid?"

Guthrie still had his back to Shaun. He was still gloating over the bunk. It might have been a sixth sense which told him what Shaun was doing. The sort of instinct which was a vital part of the armoury of a gunfighter.

Shaun did not answer. Now Guthrie turned to face him. Shaun forced himself to meet the dark, cruel eyes.

"Mebbe you were tryin' to get to that cabin first? Put that idea out of your head, kid. Nothin' is goin' to spoil the surprise I plan for this Catsfoot hombre. But I ain't in any hurry. If I wait another hour he'll be asleep and that'll make it just so much easier."

Wait till Catsfoot was asleep ... ! The sheer ruthless horror of it forced Shaun to a wild decision.

He was still partly out of the room, standing in the doorway. It was Brent's habit to lock it when he left the building and the key was in the outside. It might be possible....

Shaun made a twisting, backward jump. At the same time, he thrust out a hand. The door slammed shut. Now in almost total darkness, he groped for the big iron key. But at first he could not find it. His frantic fingers clawed only at the bare wood. Then the back of his hand grazed across the key. He gripped it. He was about to turn it. In another moment he *would* have turned it. But Guthrie's great weight crashed against the panels at the other side. The door lashed open, hitting Shaun full in the face. He staggered back against the wall. There was an acute pain in his nostrils and he felt blood trickling down them. His eyes were watering.

Guthrie was coming after him, snorting like a maddened bull. Shaun saw him as a vast shadow. Pressing against the wall, he tried to move away. But Guthrie followed, pace for pace. And he was keeping himself between Shaun and the outer door, so that there seemed no chance of escape.

Something touched Shaun's head and shoulders.

Something which was solid, yet moved easily enough. It appeared to be swinging.

Abruptly, Shaun realised what it was.

His father's gunbelt.

It had been put back its hook after Brent had been laid on the bunk. And the Colt "Bulldog" was in the holster.

Since Guthrie could not see clearly what was happening, Shaun thought that he ought to be able to pull the gun from the holster—and to use it. He could scarcely miss if he aimed at that vast shadow which was only a few feet away.

Shaun put out a hand. This time he was lucky, he contacted the gun butt immediately. It felt cold, reassuring. He lifted it an inch. Then he let it drop back in the holster.

In a vital, life-saving flash, he knew the truth.

Guthrie would be certain to fire first if he tried to use that gun.

The reason was simple.

The Colt "Bulldog"—like all revolvers of the period—had a single-action mechanism. The hammer did not cock under trigger pressure. It had to be thumbed back and that always produced a clear, unmistakeable clicking sound. Guthrie would react to that sound. He would draw and shoot before Shaun could tighten his forefinger.

But there was another way....

Shaun whipped the belt off the hook. He gave it a twist round his wrist, so that it hung with gun and holster at the bottom, like a pendulum. Then he whirled it in a vicious arc.

He heard a thud. Then a groan. And he knew that the loaded holster had crashed against Guthrie's head. He moved closer, to strike again. But it was not necessary.

That shadow which was Guthrie was swaying like a great tree in a storm. There was a crash which made the floorboards tremble as he hit the floor. Then silence.

Shaun did not hesitate—he dare not hesitate. Guthrie was unconscious now, but he might recover within moments. In four strides, Shaun was at the outer door. Buckling the gunbelt to his waist, he looked along the main street. Lights were glowing in some of the windows, but no one was to be seen. From the saloon, which was a little way off, wild voices could be heard singing and arguing. It seemed that most of Guthrie's men were in there—drinking and not paying. Then Shaun saw the horses. There were three of them, all obviously belonging to the outfit and tethered to the hitching-rail outside the saloon. Shaun ran towards them.

They were big horses, each of them between sixteen and seventeen hands. Strong, too, with well-muscled quarters. But their hides were flaky with dust and dried sweat. They had been ridden hard that day and they had not been rubbed down.

Shaun was about to free reins of the nearest

animal when he was compelled to pull back and crouch behind its flanks. The swing doors of the saloon had opened and a couple of Guthrie's men had emerged. They were standing on the board-walk.

One of them said: "Guthrie oughta be here. He sure would like the beer and the music."

"Where is he, Al?"

"Taking a look at that tin marshal," the man called Al said, "Let's fetch him...."

"Okay, we'll do that."

They swaggered towards the marshal's office. Shaun had to move slightly to remain behind the horses. But after only a few paces the two men halted.

Al said: "Mebbe we'd better put those hosses in the stables."

"They can wait. They ain't takin' any harm."

"Yep, but Guthrie said to put 'em under cover. I guess we'd better do that right now."

"Okay. We don't want to make Guthrie sore."

They began to return in the direction of the horses. Towards where Shaun was crouching. Shaun wanted to scream in a mixture of fear and rage. With an effort, he controlled himself. And he drew his gun. But the gun was a forlorn hope. He knew that if there were any shooting, everyone in the saloon would rush out to investigate. Then there would be scarcely any chance of getting away.

The two men stepped from the board-walk.

They were within a yard of the nearest horse. Shaun prepared to dart forward—to try to hold them off with the gun while he made a getaway.

There was a crash from inside the saloon.

It was a partly muffled noise, as if a heavy table had been turned over. It was distinct above the tinkling of a piano and bawdy singing. Then, for perhaps three seconds, there was absolute silence, as if everyone in that saloon had been struck dumb. It ended with another crash and the sound of breaking glass. And a medley of fierce shouting. A brawl was beginning.

The two men did not hesitate. They forgot about the horses. Together, they rushed through the swing doors, eager to see and to join in.

As the doors opened, Shaun caught a glimpse of several men locked together in a fight. Tables lay on their sides, packs of cards were strewn over the floor.

That was all that Shaun saw. But it was enough for him to know that he had been given a perfect opportunity. Or so it seemed. Not a moment of it must be wasted.

Darting towards the hitching-rail, he freed all three reins. He swung into the saddle of a sorrel mare and pulled her head round with his left hand. His right hand was gripping the leathers of the two other animals, taking them with him as he pressed into a gallop.

He was a mile on the way to Oxby Tops before

he let the riderless horses go free. Their absence would delay pursuit. He had gained extra time.

The mare reared and whinnied. It stood almost vertically on its hind legs. The sheer unexpectedness of it unseated Shaun. He tried to grasp the saddle pommel but had not a chance of doing so. He turned a somersault over the animal's back before hitting the hard earth.

His mind was a haze. What had happened? What had caused the horse to take fright?

He heard a snarl, vicious yet subdued. Dimly he saw an outline which was long, low and powerful. He recognised it. A jaguar.

Those felines were not common in Arizona, but they occasionally wandered over the border from Mexico. They were vicious fighters, but they did not usually attack humans unless provoked or afraid. This one, Shaun realised, must have been startled by the horse while hunting. It's mood was dangerous—very dangerous.

It was circling him. And those circles were gradually becoming tighter. At any moment it might attack.

With a sweating hand he drew the gun. Lying on his stomach, he cocked the hammer.

The clicking sound made the jaguar halt. It stared at Shaun. He could see clearly only its eyes. They were green pools in the gloom. Unblinking and ruthless. And they were less than half a dozen paces away.

Shaun pressed the trigger.

Nothing happened. Nothing save another click as the hammer fell.

It was a bad cartridge. Such mis-fires were not uncommon and they were the main reason why some gunfighters used two revolvers in a double draw—it was an insurance.

Feverishly, he again cocked the gun.

And at that same moment the jaguar attacked.

It leapt high into the air, claws and fangs bared.

Shaun fired when it was descending on him. When it was directly over him and he could smell the animal's fetid breath.

The explosion and the impact of the slug seemed to jerk the jaguar back in mid-air. It twisted. Then it fell on its side, its head and shoulder hitting the small of Shaun's back.

Shaun felt a wave of hideous pain sweep across his entire body. The sudden impact was like a hammer blow. And the solid weight remained on him. He tried to twist away from it. But the attempt at movement renewed the pain so that he groaned.

He whispered to himself: "It's my spine … mebbe it's broken!"

The thought of lying there unable to move made him want to sob with terror. Now he would never reach Catsfoot. He might never be found and in that case he would die with a dead jaguar on top of him. Or, if he were found, it would almost certainly be by Guthrie's killers when the pursuit began. In either case, the future seemed hopeless.

He decided to try again.

Very gently, he attempted a half roll. There was another spasm of pain. But now it was not nearly so severe. He was able to squirm from under the weight. And Shaun knew that he had feared without cause. His spine was not broken. He knew that the pain was caused by bruised muscles and nerve shock.

Slowly, he got to his feet.

Now where was his horse? Rubbing his back, he stared around. It must be found—and found fast. He saw it. It appeared as a substantial silhouette, about twenty yards away.

Shaun approached it, but at the same time the mare moved off. Shaun stopped and the mare stopped. The animal was scared, unsure of whether to let Shaun approach.

There was only one way of dealing with that.

In a soft voice, Shaun began speaking to it. And as he spoke he slowly moved closer. This time the mare remained still. Shaun extended a hand. With the tips of his fingers he touched its mouth. It was twitching and shivering. But Shaun was able to get back into the saddle. And to set off again for Oxby Tops.

Shaun guided the mare between a narrow fringe of mesquite trees.

The animal was almost wind-blown when he emerged from them, for he had been compelled to ride it hard to make up for lost time.

But now the journey was practically over. He skirted a cluster of giant saguaro cacti. They stood like sentinels under the thin moonlight, their yellow flowers quivering in the breeze. And beyond those cacti, just over what had once been a river bed, he saw the cabin.

Here it was—the place where the legendary Catsfoot was said to be staying.

But as he looked he felt a sinking of his spirits.

No light showed from its narrow windows. Standing in the midst of rustling sagebrush, it looked exactly as it had done for years—lonely and deserted. Shaun could not help wondering whether his father's information had been right. Suppose it was all a mistake? Suppose this man called Catsfoot was not staying here? The thought wearied him more than all the dangers of the day.

Shaun rode the last few yards at a slow canter, never taking his eyes off the cabin. He dismounted opposite the sprucewood door. He hesitated, then hammered on it with a fist. There was no sound of movement from inside. No inquiring voice. He hammered again. Still no answer. He turned the handle and pushed. The door opened an inch, then stuck. Shaun thudded against it with his shoulder, but it refused to shift. It seemed that the rotting woodwork had warped against the floor.

He walked heavily to one of the two windows and tried to peer through it. It was too dark inside. He could see nothing.

So it *was* a mistake....

Shaun felt as if his spirit had shrivelled. As if the will to fight had gone because nothing was certain save defeat. He sat on the ground, his back propped against the cabin wall, and stared vacantly into black space. He did not care whether Guthrie came now or came later. Neither did he care what happened to him. He almost wanted to weep.

Then he heard a voice.

It came from very close to him. Yet the tones were so gentle, so friendly, that Shaun felt no sense of shock.

The voice was saying: "This ain't much of a way for you to spend the night, son. You'll be a whole lot more comfortable in the cabin."

A man was standing over him. A man who was very tall and slender. He was wearing stained buckskins. A wide-brimmed fedora was pulled well down over his face, so that in the poor light it was impossible to see his face. Shaun glanced at his waist. He was carrying two guns and they were slung low.

"Gee! You must be Catsfoot!" Shaun said, jumping to his feet.

"That's what folks call me, son. But how do you know my name? And who are you?"

"I'm Shaun Brent... my father told me to find you."

"Brent ... I seem to remember that name."

"My pop's Herb Brent and he's the marshal at Gloryrise."

"Herb! Why I knew him years back when I was in Tucson. But I didn't know he was in these parts and I didn't know he had a boy."

Shaun said urgently: "I've come to warn you, Catsfoot, there's trouble comin' this way! A bunch of gun-slingers are comin' out to fix you and they..."

Shaun felt an arm go round his shoulders. And that gentle voice said: "You can tell me about it in the cabin, Shaun. If anyone's coming this way I'll hear them when they go through the mesquites. That's when I heard you, so I just pulled out— so I could see what was happening without anyone seeing me. I sure am sorry if I've scared you."

Catsfoot took hold of the door handle. He had to push very hard and it opened reluctantly, with squeaking and scraping. Shaun remained in the threshold, unsure of his bearings, while Catsfoot went inside. There was a splutter of flame and suddenly an open oil lamp was spreading a soft light through the cabin.

There was scarcely any furniture in the place. The lamp was set on an old wooden crate in the middle of the bare floor. Against one wall was a sheepskin sleeping-bag and a saddle which was apparently being used as a pillow. Harness leathers were piled in a corner.

A few books were laid neatly on a window shelf. One of them was open, as if it was being read. It occurred to Shaun that they were somehow out of place in this bare atmosphere. But, having taken a quick glance round, he forgot about them. He was anxious to look at Catsfoot.

And the words his father had used came back as clearly as if they were being spoken again.

"There's a kind of magic about him...."

That was what Herb Brent had said of Catsfoot.

It was true. It was something which could not be explained. But it could not be missed.

The face which was smiling at Shaun was unlike any he had ever seen before. It was not the rough-hewn sort of face which was to be seen everywhere in the new territories. The features were finely formed. There was kindness and laughter in his blue-grey eyes.

He had taken his fedora off, showing thick and fair hair. It curled down to his shoulders.

This very tall man in buckskins made Shaun think of a poet or an artist. And yet there was obviously much more to him than that. Strength of character was there, too. Shaun sensed that the face could harden in a moment. Physical strength showed in the wide shoulders, which contrasted with the tapering slenderness of the rest of his body.

Automatically, Shaun looked again at his guns. They hung from a single belt which was buckled tightly over the loose-fitting buckskin jacket. The butts were thin and of smooth wood. Shaun recognised them as the popular .44 "Dragoons."

Shaun realised that Catsfoot was talking to him. He was saying: "I guess I can't ask you to sit down, Shaun—unless you want to use the floor."

"I'm okay, thanks," Shaun said, staring up at him.

"Now suppose you tell me what all the trouble's about, right from the beginning."

Shaun told him. Once, as he described the shooting of his father, his voice broke and he could not suppress a sob. In front of other men he might have felt ashamed of breaking down. But before Catsfoot it did not seem to matter. Already Shaun felt as if he were with an old and trusted friend.

Catsfoot was silent for a while after Shaun had finished. The smile had gone from his eyes. Eventually he said: "I'll help all I can, but mebbe I won't be able to do much. Guthrie's taken charge of Gloryrise and he holds all the aces."

"But Pop says you can get the ordinary folk to stand together against Guthrie's outfit."

"That won't be easy, Shaun. Anyway, it's a

big responsibility asking peaceful people to stand up against a mob of gun-slingers."

That answer surprised Shaun. It was far from what he had expected. He said: "But you've got a lot of advantages, Catsfoot."

"I have? Name one of them."

"There's your guns. Pop says you're even faster than Guthrie."

Catsfoot looked down at his .44s as if he hated them. Then he crossed to the window shelf where the books were laid. He asked: "Have you been wondering why I'm in this shack?"

"I have—and I think Pop's been wonderin', too."

"I'm resting, Shaun. You see, for years I've been guiding wagon trains all over the territories, mostly through Indian country. That kind of work weighs heavy on a man, because the safety of so many people depend on him. And before that, I was a scout for the Federal Armies in the Civil War. In all that time I've hardly had one clear day to myself—not till now. It so happened that a week ago I signed a routine contract to take a wagon train from Tucson to Carson City, in Nevada. Then I heard that another scout was in need of the job. He's a good man and I was able to let him take over. I was glad to be able to take things easy for a while. Then I remembered this shack and came to it."

Shaun scratched his head.

"But why come to a tumbledown place like this? Why didn't you go into Gloryrise and stop at the town hotel?"

Catsfoot hesitated. He coloured slightly beneath his tan. Then he pointed to the books.

"Can you read, Shaun?"

"Yes..."

"I mean, can you read well?"

Shaun was slightly confused. He said: "I guess so. We have classes in the town mission hall."

"You're lucky. When I was a kid I never had a chance to learn, but I always wanted to be able to open a book and understand what's in it. Then, way back, I once had a lawyer travelling with one of my wagon trains and he gave me a start by showing me the alphabet. After that, I started to teach myself. It hasn't been so easy and there hasn't been much time for it, neither. But I've worked up so that right now I'm on proper lit ... lit ..."

He stumbled over the word. Shaun said quietly: "Literature?"

"Yep, that's right. But I read kind of slow and I have to say the words as I go along. When folks see me doing that they think it's kind of crazy and they laugh behind my back. That's why I wanted to be alone. Do you understand?"

Shaun did understand. And he realised that he had glimpsed a new side to Catsfoot's character.

It explained why even his way of speaking was not so rough as was usual.

Shaun moved closer to Catsfoot. He looked at the book which lay open. It was Nathaniel Hawthorne's *Tanglewood Tales.* Next to it he was surprised and pleased to see Herman Melville's sea story *Redburn,* which Shaun himself had only recently finished reading for the third time.

"I'm real proud of those books," Catsfoot was saying. "I had them freighted all the way from New York. They cost me a lot, but they're worth every dollar. They're showing me a new world I knew nothing about."

Shaun had to turn away and blink hard. He blurted: "I'm sorry … it just isn't right bringin' all this trouble to you when you're tryin' to improve yourself and forget about being a trail scout and a gunfighter!"

"Gunfighter? I don't like being called that, Shaun."

"Gee, Catsfoot, I didn't mean it the wrong way! But Pop told me how you can draw."

"I've tried to fix it so I can use my guns faster than any man alive," Catsfoot said simply. "I figure I've succeeded. Anyway, no one's beaten me yet. But I ain't specially proud of that, Shaun. I'm not a top-gun because I want to kill folks or scare them. To me, it's just a tool of trade I must have. You see, a trail scout has to be able to pro-tect the people in his care and when I was no older than you I decided two things. I made up my mind to guide the wagon trains. And I wanted to be sure no thug with a fast draw was goin' to harm any of the folks who trusted me. I use my guns when I have to—but I've never liked it and I never will."

"I know that," Shaun said. "I knew it from the time I first saw you outside this cabin. Right now, I want..."

Catsfoot put up a hand for silence. Shaun listened, could hear nothing.

But Catsfoot said: "Our visitors are on the way. They're ridin' through the mesquites."

"You sure?"

"Yep, and by the sound I'd say there's quite a few of them."

"Then we'll have to move fast!"

"Where to?" Catsfoot asked, smiling again.

"Any place—but we've got to get out of here!"

Catsfoot shook his head.

"That wouldn't help any. Wherever we went, they'd soon pick up our trail in the thick sage. Anyway, there's no sense in trying to run. I figure Mister Guthrie and me have got to meet some time and it might as well be right now."

"But you won't just be meetin' Guthrie!" Shaun almost shouted. "The rest of 'em are killers, too. They won't give you a chance ... not now they've heard you're a top-gun!"

Catsfoot said softly: "I'll make my own chances, if I have to."

Now Shaun heard the approaching horses.

Catsfoot dropped his hands on his "Dragoons." At first, Shaun thought that he was going to draw them. But instead he thumbed back the hammers. Then he moved till he was against a wall and out of line of the windows. He gestured to Shaun.

"Stand by that corner," he said. "I want you close to me—but not too close."

Shaun obeyed, his heart thudding like a trip-hammer. The horsemen seemed to be circling the cabin. He heard muffled shouting from some of them.

The hoofbeats became gradually slower, yet louder. Finally, they ceased. There was a clink of several bridle chains just outside the door. And a creaking of stirrup leathers as men swung out of saddles.

A bellowing voice boomed through the cabin. "Is a critter name of Catsfoot in there?"

Shaun whispered: "That's Guthrie!"

Catsfoot gave him a quick nod as he called back: "Yep, I'm here and waiting."

"Mebbe you have the kid with you?"

"Mebbe I have. Why don't you come in and find out?"

"I'll do that...."

Guthrie tried to push open the door. But the

warped wood stuck. His heavy breathing could be heard. There was a crash as his shoulder slammed against it and it was jerked open.

And Guthrie stamped into the cabin. Four others followed him. Among them, Shaun recognised the man named Al. They crowded in the middle of the floor, staring at Catsfoot, hands near their holsters. There was an ugly blue bruise on the side of Guthrie's head, just in front of the left ear.

Catsfoot stared back at them. He was standing with one foot slightly in front of the other, legs apart. His arms hung at his sides. Only his flat open hands hinted at what he was expecting. The rest of him seemed to be completely relaxed.

Guthrie's eyes suddenly became slits.

He said: "I overheard the marshal talkin' about you, Catsfoot. He said you were a fast gun."

"That's right—I guess I am."

"He said you were faster than me."

"Mebbe that's right, too."

"There's no man faster than me! I'm Guthrie: does than mean anything to you?"

"It means a lot."

"I'm glad of it. Tell me what you've heard."

"Mostly that you're a dirty, thieving killer and you've got a crowd of the same sort behind you. There are too many of your kind in Arizona right now and the territory won't be fit for decent folks to live in till we've got rid of you."

Guthrie's breathing became faster and heavier, his huge chest rising and falling.

"That's big talk, Catsfoot. There was another guy talked to me that way this very day. He was lucky—he's still alive. I figure you ain't goin' to be so lucky. I'm goin' to nail you, then I'll see to the kid!"

"You can leave Shaun out of it, Guthrie. If you feel like drawing on me, go right ahead. But I guess even you stop short of killing kids."

Guthrie stretched his lips across bad teeth.

"He's big as kids go, so he can take what's comin' from me. I owe him plenty. But first you're goin' to collect, Catsfoot. You ready to draw?"

The men with Guthrie shuffled aside, out of the line of fire. In that cabin, there was no more than half a dozen paces between Catsfoot and Guthrie.

Catsfoot said: "I'll be ready when Shaun's out of here. This is no place for him, Guthrie. Let him ride back to Gloryrise."

"Quit stallin' for time, Catsfoot! It won't help you none! The kid stays right here—and you're goin' to collect a hot slug!"

"So that's the way..."

Shaun did not hear any more.

For it was at that moment that he saw it.

Saw something tiny, yet deadly. Something

which slid out of Al's sleeve. It settled in Al's right hand. There it was almost completely concealed.

It was a Derringer.

A single-shot Derringer pistol—sometimes called "the gambler's gun." Just a dwarf of a weapon, weight only eleven ounces, barrel length a mere three inches. But at short range it could be as lethal as a Colt.

Al was aiming it at Catsfoot's head. But he was holding it so that it was practically impossible for Catsfoot to see it. Shaun saw the contemptible truth—Guthrie had set up Al as a cover-gun. Al was preparing to shoot the moment before Catsfoot drew.

Shaun gave a crazed shout. And as he shouted, he hurtled at Al.

He heard a sharp, vicious crack from the Derringer. Like a whip. Then he was falling backwards and Al was on top of him. They were falling across the wooden crate. They were crashing against the top of Guthrie's legs.

Guthrie....

His gun was out. But he had not fired it. Instead, he was bellowing a warning as he reeled partly off balance.

In the centre of the ghastly chaos, Shaun knew the reason.

It was the lamp.

The lamp had turned over. A deep river of oil

from it had streaked across the floor, making a tall wall of lurid flame between Guthrie and Catsfoot. Catsfoot....

His guns were out, too. But he had not used them, either. He was slowly folding to the ground. Blood was flowing over his face.

CHAPTER THREE

IN THE SAGE

OIL was burning.

Then oil and wood were burning. Together, they were sending up billows of black smoke.

Pushed by the draught from the open door, the river of flame swelled into a pond. And the pond was bloating into a fiery sea. A sea which in a few moments would be consuming the entire floor. The speed of it all temporarily shrivelled the spirit, turned the mind to a dazed mush.

Shaun writhed across the crate, Al over him. He glimpsed Catsfoot again. Now Catsfoot was huddled on the boards. His eyes were shut.

A force like a battering ram hit Shaun's chest. It was Al's fist. The power of it made him groan, made him wonder whether he was being driven through the top of the crate. But suddenly the weight of Al's body was gone. Al was running for the door. Guthrie and the others followed Al—taking leaping strides through the flames.

And Shaun became aware of the heat. It was at his ankles and his face. But most of all, it was scorching his lungs.

He dragged himself to his knees, then stood on

the crate. That crate itself was beginning to burn in the midst of the blaze.

The fire had not yet reached Catsfoot, but it would soon do so.

Shaun jumped. Thrusting with both legs, arching his body forward, he sprang over the flames to the ribbon of clear floor where Catsfoot lay. As he rushed through the hot air he heard the crate crash on to its side.

He hit the wall with his outstretched hands. Instinctively he pushed to prevent injuring his face, and he staggered back to the edge of the fire. But he recovered and bent over Catsfoot.

Catsfoot was completely still and the blood was thick over his forehead and cheeks. He might be dead, but there was no time to examine him. No time for anything except to try to get him out of the inferno.

But how?

They were now entirely cut off from the door. The blaze was reaching up as well as out and to attempt to move through it dragging an unconscious man would mean a certain and awful end.

There was a window. The window under which the books were laid out. It was in the wall and about three feet away. Catsfoot had moved from directly in front of it just before Guthrie arrived.

Shaun reeled towards it.

It was a single, fixed pane. He crashed the butt of his Colt "Bulldog" against it. A shower of glass splattered out. At the same time, the cool night air came in, soothing his lungs. More blows with the gun and there was an opening through which a man might be pushed. But small pieces of jagged glass were still embedded in the casement. Catsfoot would suffer deep wounds if he lay over them. Shaun pulled off his jacket, folded it twice and spread it over the dangerous base.

Then he returned to Catsfoot.

But, away from the window, the heat was now almost impossible to bear. And smoke made his eyes stream so that he could scarcely see. It was like being in a furnace.

Retching, choking, Shaun worked mostly by sense of touch. He got his hands under Catsfoot's arms, dragged him under the window. Now came the vital problem—how to lift him through it. There was only one possible way and Shaun used it. He held Catsfoot's wrists, then crouched with his back to him. A pull, and the upper part of Catsfoot's body was resting against Shaun's shoulders. Shaun tried to straighten up with the weight over him. It was a brief but desperate struggle. During it, Shaun thought that his spine would break, for although Catsfoot was slender he was also very tall and heavy with hard muscle. But somehow—he never quite knew how—he managed it. With his head resting against the shelf and using his back as a platform, Shaun forced Catsfoot forward until he was balanced over the bottom of the opening.

Now Catsfoot was hanging face down, partly out of the cabin. Another push and he would drop clear of it. But that drop was all of four feet. It, too, could be dangerous. Shaun realised that despite the torture of the heat and smoke, he must work slowly. He gripped the bottom of Catsfoot's saddle boots and pressed gently. As the weight started to slide, Shaun pulled back so that it descended gently. He let go when, looking through the window, he saw that Catsfoot's head and shoulders were already resting in the sage.

For the moment, Catsfoot was clear of the flames.

Shaun was about to follow when he saw two objects glitter on the floor. They were Catsfoot's guns. The fire was within inches of them. For some reason which Shaun could not explain, he knew that they had to be saved. He ran to them and pushed them under his belt. Then, all but blinded, he got back to the window. He pulled himself over the ledge, swayed there, then dropped beside Catsfoot.

Here the air was so comparatively cold that it hurt. Shaun's coughing became worse, shaking his entire body. But it suddenly passed. His eyes cleared, so did his head.

He was sprawled beside Catsfoot, both of them close against the outer wall. Smoke was streaming through chinks and slits in the spruce wood. Soon the entire cabin would be ablaze and probably much of the sage around it, too. He must drag Catsfoot well clear. But abruptly he knew that he could not do so. Not right now. Every muscle was aching and trembling. All the strength had gone from him. His brain told him to move— to seize Catsfoot once again and pull him from danger. But his body refused to obey.

It was then that Catsfoot groaned. Just a short and soft sound, such as a man might make in sleep.

But to Shaun it confirmed a hope. It answered a question which he had hardly dared to ask. He thought: "It was all worth it! He's alive! He might have..."

There was a twitching round Catsfoot's mouth. His eyelids flickered, then with startling suddenness they were open. He was staring up at Shaun. For a second or two, his expression was vacant, his whole blood-covered face slack. But it became taut as recollection flooded back. He raised a hand to his head then looked at the reddened fingers. Then he sat upright.

"By the feel of it," he said weakly, "I'm the luckiest man in the territory. Seems like a slug's grazed my skull... I guess it was the hombre with the Derringer."

"You saw him! I thought you couldn't possibly do that 'cause he brought it down his sleeve."

"I saw what was happening when you rushed

at him, but I couldn't shoot because you were in the way. I've got to thank you, Shaun...."

Shaun interrupted, gesturing to the cabin.

"Never mind that—we've got to get away from here."

Catsfoot rose unsteadily to his feet. With his sweatcloth he wiped some of the blood from his forehead and cheeks. He glanced through the smashed window to the inferno within.

"Did you haul me out of that?"

"Yep, but the fire wasn't so bad then."

The walls were now thoroughly alight. There was a series of thuds and a cascade of sparks as part of the roof fell in.

Catsfoot said: "I never did own very much, but most all I had was in there. It seems like I've lost everything except my horse ... my saddle and leathers, my blankets, my guns and my books have gone. You know something? I figure I'll miss those books more than all the rest."

Shaun pulled the pair of "Dragoons" from his belt.

"I'm sorry about the books, but your guns are here."

Catsfoot took them from him. He spun the cylinders, then he dropped them in their holsters. When he spoke again there was a new edge to his voice. It was brittle. It was straining under fury.

"I sure am glad you saved those," he said. "I've work for them! Work concerning Guthrie and it isn't going to wait. It looks like he's left us both for dead in the cabin, but he's going to have a jolt."

"But you'll *have* to wait a while, Catsfoot! Mebbe that's only a skull graze you've got, but it must have shaken you up a lot. You'll have to lay up some place for a few days."

Catsfoot shook his head and touched the wound.

"I'm okay. I've stopped bleeding, so we'll start riding into Gloryrise right now. It seems your horse has gone, but mine's grazing way back from here on a long tether line. It's strong enough to carry us both."

"You'll need harness."

"I can fix a bit and halter out of the tether rope."

Shaun was still anxious. He tried again to dissuade Catsfoot.

"Let's wait just one whole day! You *need* to rest and..."

The words died in Shaun's throat.

Amid the red glow of destruction, something strange happened to Catsfoot. Something almost satanic.

There was a vibrating crash. It came from both of his hands. And only then did Shaun see that the guns were in them. He had been watching all the time, but his eyes had not been able to follow the draw. Just as previously he had been unable to follow Guthrie's draw....

Catsfoot's guns were aimed at a point in the red-tinted sagebrush, at least forty yards away. But, so far as Shaun could make out in the light from the blaze, there was nothing there—no possible target. He blinked at Catsfoot, bewildered and a little afraid.

"Go and take a look at it," Catsfoot said, and each word was like a chip of flint.

"But... but what is it? Who's there?"

"See for yourself. You won't come to any harm."

Strength was returning to Shaun. He ran to the place. There he halted for a moment, peered down and gasped. Then he rushed back.

"It's... it's a rattlesnake!"

"I know it."

"You've blown its head off! But how did you see it in that long sage?"

Catsfoot was relaxed and smiling again.

"Never mind how," he said softly, "I did it, and that's what matters. Now do you think I'm in a condition to handle Guthrie?"

Shaun hesitated. He knew that in the space of a few hours he had seen in action two of the fastest guns on earth. But which was the fastest of the two? Which of them had that vital edge (it could be no more than a tiny fraction of a second) which would mean the difference between life and death? Herb Brent was sure it was Catsfoot. But Shaun was level-headed enough to know that a man usually believed what he wanted to believe. All justice, all humanity demanded that Catsfoot should be faster. But that was no guarantee. In any case, Guthrie had already shown that he was not prepared to risk a level fight with Catsfoot. When they met again, there would be another cover-gun....

It seemed that Catsfoot knew what Shaun was thinking. For he said: "Next time *I'll* pick the place where I meet Guthrie and no one will get a chance to pull a Derringer out of his sleeve."

A lizard rolled its eyelids and glided under a board-walk. A carrion bird, probing the garbage, gave an angry squawk before flapping away. Both were disturbed by the horse with two riders. It was unusual for them to be disturbed by anything at this hour in Gloryrise.

It was the hour when departing night was lingering with arriving daylight and the whole town slept.

The horse, champing on an improvised rope bit, was reined in outside the marshal's office. Catsfoot and Shaun jumped from its bare back. They stood by the hitching-rail, looking at the main street. It was a street of new and ugly scars. The saloon windows were smashed. A table was hanging out of one of them. The door of the mercantile store was wrenched from its hinges. Much of the stock was scattered about the sidewalk. Empty bottles were everywhere. In the centre of the street someone had left a stirrup boot, complete with spur.

Shaun gave a weary sigh.

"It sure does look bad," he said, "but I guess it's only the beginning. I've heard how Guthrie's men do much worse things to towns before they leave. And this was such a good place. Mebbe we were too lucky. We never even had trouble with the Apaches. In fact, we do some trading with their camp near here. Now it's ... it's awful...."

Catsfoot nodded. Then he pointed to the hotel at the end of the street and asked: "Is that where the outfit are living?"

"Yep. They've taken the whole place over."

"I guess they'll be sleeping nice and soft, thinking I was killed in that cabin and probably you, too. They're going to get one big surprise. But before that happens I want to have a talk with your father."

Shaun led the way into the building and through to the rear room. The lamp was still burning there. Automatically, Shaun's eyes went to the bunk where the bandaged figure lay. Herb Brent was sleeping. A woman, fat and elderly, was dozing in a chair beside him. Shaun recognised Mrs. Hepple, who was well known in Gloryrise for her nursing skill. She awoke with a start and gave a smile of relief when she saw Shaun.

"Am I glad to see you, honey!" she said. "We've all been fearin' for you."

"I'm fine, Mrs. Hepple, and I'm glad you're helpin' to look after Pop. How is he?"

"He'll be okay, but it'll be a long while before he's movin' around again. But say... who's your tall friend in the buckskins?"

"This is Catsfoot. He's a trail scout and he's here to help us."

Catsfoot glided forward, hand outstretched.

"I'm glad to know you, ma'am."

Mrs. Hepple took the hand and stared up at him in wonder.

"Catsfoot ... ! Say, I've heard that name before. Ain't you the man who's reckoned to be a top-gun?"

"I guess that's me, ma'am, but I don't like to be known for my gunplay. But listen, I want to talk to Brent. Would it be okay for you to wake him?"

She looked doubtful.

"I ain't so sure. Y'see, it's a bad thing to rouse a sick man from his rest."

"I don't like the idea myself, ma'am, but it's kind of urgent."

Brent solved the difficulty for them. He awoke suddenly, blinking at Catsfoot then at Shaun. He mumbled something and tried to sit up, but could scarcely move an inch.

"It's Catsfoot! So you found him okay

Shaun! I … I sure am glad to see you, Catsfoot. Mebbe you've heard what's goin' on here?"

"I've heard," Catsfoot said, bending over the bunk and laying a hand gently on Brent's shoulder.

"I did hear you was at the cabin on Oxby Tops... can you do anything for us, Catsfoot? Can you save this town before it's pulled to bits?"

Despite his weakness, there was a desperate urgency about Brent. Sweat was glistening on his face and it was soaking through his bandages.

"I can't do much by myself, Brent, but I figure I can do a lot if the folks in the burgh will stand with me."

"That's what I meant! That's what I told Shaun you'd say!"

Catsfoot sat on the edge of the bunk.

"I'm going to ask you to do one thing to help," he said, "and after that you can forget just about everything except getting better from that wound."

Brent seemed puzzled.

"Sure, I'll do anything y'want—but what *can* I do, trussed up like this?"

"You can swear me in as temporary marshal."

"Temporary marshal! Yep, I guess I have legal power to do that, seein' I can't do the job m'self."

Catsfoot asked: "Can a temporary marshal appoint his own deputies?"

"He sure can. Under Federal Law, a temporary has the same powers as a full marshal, except that he can't hold office for more than six weeks without permission from a circuit judge."

"I won't need six weeks," Catsfoot said. "For better or worse, I figure this'll all be settled in a lot less than six days."

Mrs. Hepple interrupted to wipe the sweat off Brent's face. Then, looking straight up from his pillow, Brent said: "I don't want you to get this wrong, Catsfoot. Y'see, Guthrie and his outfit don't care nothin' about whether a man's wearin' a silver badge. It just won't help you any."

Catsfoot stood up and pointed towards the main street.

"Out there," he said, "you've got a lot of ordinary decent people. People who respect the law, and that's the way it ought to be. But right now, they're scared. I don't blame 'em. They've seen law in this burgh fold up in front of their eyes. That's no disrespect to you, Brent, because you've done more than anyone had a right to expect of one man. But they've got to know that the law's back in town and that they are *part* of it. That's why I want to be temporary marshal, and it's why I intend to swear in as deputies as many of the townsfolk as are willing. If it's all legal, I figure enough of them will follow me to get rid of Guthrie. But they might not be so anxious about getting into what'd look like a gun brawl."

Brent said: "You're right … get my Bible, Shaun."

Shaun went into the office and took the Bible from the desk. He handed it to Catsfoot, who then repeated after Brent the oath of a marshal.

When that was done, Brent said to Shaun: "Give me m'badge."

Shaun took the badge from his father's coat, which was hanging over the back of the chair, and handed it to him.

"Come closer, Catsfoot," Brent said.

Catsfoot leaned over the bunk. With fumbling hands, Brent pinned the silver star to the buckskin jacket.

"Now the job's yours," Brent whispered. "I figure this town's just got itself the best marshal in all the new territories...." He closed his eyes, wearied by the strain of the last few minutes. Then, just before he drifted into another deep sleep, he murmured: "Get Guthrie, Catsfoot. Whatever happens, get Guthrie.... When he's out of the way, that mob'll break up and Arizona'll be a cleaner place...."

Catsfoot straightened the blankets over him. Then he turned to Mrs. Hepple.

"I need your help, ma'am."

She looked surprised and pleased.

"You'll have it, Catsfoot."

"Will you get the word around town that I want every man who's willing to be deputised to be in this office right away?"

"I sure will do that."

"It's got to be done fast. I must have them in here before the town's astir. Right now, Guthrie and his outfit are sleeping in the hotel and I want to catch them that way."

Mrs. Hepple said: "I'll go to my brother first. He'll soon spread the word to the right men."

Shaun interrupted. "I'll help. I know the right men, too."

But Catsfoot shook his head.

"You've got to stay right here with me, Shaun. If you go out, there's just a chance that one of Guthrie's mob might be around and see you. They think most likely you died in the cabin with me and I want them to go on thinking that for another half hour—until we surprise them in the hotel."

Shaun knew that Catsfoot was right. And at the same time he realised that Catsfoot was already acting on a plan which could end the terror in Gloryrise without bloodshed—or without much bloodshed. Even a small number of determined men would have a tremendous advantage if they could get into the hotel while Guthrie's outfit was still sleeping there....

Mrs. Hepple was pulling on her poke-bonnet. As she moved towards the door she said to Catsfoot: "There's a can of water in that corner. You'd better use it to clean up that head graze of yours."

Then she whisked out, long skirts rustling.

Shaun looked at his father. His eyes were tight-shut and he was breathing easily. His gaze travelled to Catsfoot. He was bending over the can, dashing water over his face and his long, fair hair.

Catsfoot was drying himself when he said: "Is that your pop's gun you're wearing, Shaun?"

"Yep, I took it when..."

"I remember now, you told me. But I'd rather you didn't wear it, son."

"You don't want me to wear it!"

"That's right."

"But why not? I know how to shoot and I could need it when we all go to the hotel."

"I'm sorry, Shaun, but you won't be going to the hotel with the rest of us. You've done mighty well and you've got more courage than most men. But you're not a man yet and I'm not going to see you risk your skin any more. I want you to stay right here and take that gun off."

"But I told you, I can shoot!"

"Can you shoot as well as your pop?"

"No, but..."

"He wasn't good enough, so how would you make out? Listen Shaun, from now on a gun won't be any use to you, but it might run you into a whole lot of trouble. Even Guthrie's mob wouldn't try to draw on an unarmed kid. But they would if he was waving a 'Bulldog' around. Get me?"

Shaun felt humiliated and resentful. He tried to argue.

"Can I wear it if I promise not to use it?"

"Why wear a gun if you can't use it? That'd be more dangerous than ever."

"Look, Catsfoot, I..."

But suddenly his annoyance vanished. Catsfoot had glided towards him. Now he was standing over him and smiling. He was saying: "I know how you feel, Shaun. I'm not trying to make you small. Y'see, it's because I owe you a lot that I want you to play safe from now on. It's not going to help me if I have to watch you as well as Guthrie, is it? Anyway, you've got your pop to think about. He's going to be sick for quite a time and he's going to need you. So you'll do like I say, won't you?"

Shaun smiled back. He had to.

"I'm sorry. I guess I was gettin' big ideas."

"Nothing wrong with..."

He broke off as a scream reached them. A trembling, frenzied scream mingled with sobs. It came from the main street.

Catsfoot and Shaun rushed to the outer door.

They saw Mrs. Hepple. She was running towards them, tears flowing down her face. And Guthrie was standing on the opposite board-walk. Most of his outfit were with him.

CHAPTER FOUR

TYRANTS OF GLORYRISE

THERE was a moment when Shaun's mind was almost blank—it was reeling under shock and horror. Catsfoot's voice steadied him. Catsfoot had moved to the outer edge of the board-walk. His arms were hanging easily at his sides. His eyes never left Guthrie as he said to Mrs. Hepple: "Have you been harmed, ma'am?"

She staggered up to him.

"Not... not me... it's..."

"Then don't distress yourself by telling me now, ma'am. You go inside and rest. I figure Guthrie and I can clear this up."

"They... they..."

"Please go in the office, ma'am."

Sobbing, she did so. Shaun knew that he ought to follow her. But he felt compelled to remain beside Catsfoot, to know what had happened and to see what was about to happen.

Guthrie was lounging on the board-walk directly opposite. His men were clustered on each side of him. Thumbs pushed under his gun belt, he was grinning as he stared at Catsfoot across the main street, where the newly rising sun was casting stark shadows. At each end of that street a few knots of townsfolk were lurking, ready to rush back into their homes. Some of them were still wearing nightclothes.

Guthrie bellowed: "It's nice to meet you again, Catsfoot. I was real worried about you in that cabin—too bad I couldn't stay and help. And say, you've got y'self a marshal's badge! Now ain't that nice! Y'look kind of smart!"

There was a gust of laughter from the others. The same sort of laughter which they had directed at Brent the previous day.

Catsfoot did not seem to raise his voice above talking pitch. But every word carried clearly as he asked: "What have you done to make that lady weep, Guthrie?"

"I just told her about her brother."

"Her brother... what about him?"

"I told her how we've got him in the hotel with half a dozen other folks. They're all being looked after real good."

"Go on, Guthrie ... you've got more to tell me."

Guthrie's grin deepened.

"I sure have. Mebbe I ought to tell you right from the start then you won't need to ask a lot of questions."

"Mebbe you'd better," Catsfoot said, "and you might as well warn those slugs round you not to try to draw on me while you're talking. I'll use my guns if any of them stirs a finger."

"Nobody'll draw on you, Catsfoot. It ain't necessary. From now on you're goin' to do just like I say. You're goin' to take orders from me, even if you have become the marshal! How d'you like that?"

A faint and grim smile showed at the corners of Catsfoot's mouth. His eyes were cold, unblinking.

"I don't like it and I don't believe it, but I'm still waiting to hear you explain."

"Okay, here it is. First, we didn't ride straight back here when we got out of the cabin. No sir, we stuck around for a time, close by the mesquites. We watched the kid push you clear of the fire. We saw it all and we didn't move off till you started to wake up."

"You could have killed me then, Guthrie. Why didn't you?"

"I nearly did," Guthrie said. "Then I got to thinkin' of something a whole lot better. I figured you were the sort of hombre who'd try to play the hero by comin' into town and makin' trouble. So I decided to make you eat dirt, Catsfoot. You've got y'self a big reputation and I saw how to end that. I saw how to fix you so folks'll only laugh when your name comes up. I guess that's even better than puttin' a slug in you."

Catsfoot said: "I think I can figure out the rest—but you tell it yourself."

"It was easy—we just took a few of the nice,

peaceful townsfolk out of their beds in the night and locked 'em in a hotel room with some of my men standin' over them. We did it the quiet way, so there was no alarm. It seems that woman's brother was one of 'em."

"And, what are you aiming to do with them?"

"That's for you and the rest of the folks to decide. They won't be harmed, so long as everyone does just like we say. But if anybody so much as starts to look tough at any of my outfit ... why, somethin' bad'll happen to those hombres we've got in the hotel. Somethin' *real* bad! Y'see what I mean?"

Catsfoot took a step forward on to the dusty, bottle-littered road. He stood beside his un-saddled horse.

"You mean," he said, "you're holding helpless people as hostages and you'll kill them if anyone stands up to you?"

"You catch on real fast, Catsfoot. It's this way —if my men in the hotel hear just one shot fired they have orders to finish the prisoners. Finish all of 'em. So you can't argue with me. Not unless you want to kill those folks and I don't figure you do."

There was a heavy silence. It was broken when Catsfoot asked: "You talked about making folks laugh at me. How d'you figure you can do that?"

"That won't be so hard. *Y'can begin by givin' me your guns!*"

Guthrie gave a snarling emphasis to the last words. And he repeated them: "Give me your guns, Catsfoot!"

Catsfoot leaned against the horse's flank.

"I've never given my guns up to any man and I don't aim to start now."

"There's always a first time for everything, Catsfoot. Right now, you've got to hand your guns to me. D'you know what I'll do if you refuse?"

"What'll you do, Guthrie?"

"I'll draw on you."

"You will? You figure you can out-draw me?"

"I'm durned certain of it. But one other thing's certain, too—when my men in the hotel hear the shootin' they'll get busy on the prisoners! Like I told you, it'll be their signal!"

Listening and watching, Shaun knew that Catsfoot was in a hideous trap. There seemed to be no escape from it, for it had been prepared with fiendish ingenuity. Shaun raced through each point in his mind, hoping to see a loophole yet knowing that there was none.

First, a handful of townsfolk were being held under guard in the hotel....

Those guards had orders to shoot them if they heard any gun play in Gloryrise. So even if Catsfoot were to outdraw Guthrie, the sound of that shot would cause the deaths of the prisoners.

Catsfoot could not draw. He would have to suffer the humiliation of surrendering his Colts. Then he would be utterly helpless....

Catsfoot pushed himself away from the horse. With his long, gliding steps he walked to the centre of the road and there he halted.

"You can have my guns," he said to Guthrie.

"I figured you'd see it that way. But I ain't takin' chances with you! You've got to do every-thing I say and do it nice and slow... now loosen your leg cords."

Catsfoot bent down. He unknotted the cords which secured his holsters to his legs.

"That's fine," Guthrie said. "Next, you've got to put your hands *under* the holsters."

Catsfoot did that.

"Tip the holsters over."

Slowly, Catsfoot tipped them till the guns fell to his feet. Guthrie's animal face was stretched into a grin of perfect pleasure.

"You're goin' to bring those Colts to me," he said. "I ain't pickin' them up. You'll hold 'em by the barrels—get it? By the *barrels!* Then when you've given 'em to me, you'll take off that marshal's badge, throw it in the dust and stand on it! After that, I'll have some more things for you to do that folks'll remember."

Catsfoot retrieved the guns from the ground,

hands round the barrels, the butts held forward. He moved towards Guthrie. He mounted the board-walk where Guthrie stood.

"Here you are," he said. "Mebbe you're satisfied now."

Guthrie gave deep chuckle.

"No I ain't satisfied. This is only the..."

Something happened to those guns. Something unearthly.

They were spinning in the air. Spinning like a pair of glittering wheels. But not for long. Just for the merest fraction of a moment.

Then....

Catsfoot was no longer holding them by the barrels. Those barrels were being pressed into the front of Guthrie's neck. And there was a simultaneous click as the two hammers were thumbed back.

But Guthrie's gun was out, too.

His single "Frontier" had moved as fast as Catsfoot's brace of "Dragoons." It was cocked and it was being pushed against the centre of Catsfoot's stomach.

Shaun had to close his eyes. And with them closed, he waited for the shattering explosions which would mean the certain end of the two men —and of the prisoners held in the hotel.

But no explosion came.

Shaun forced himself to look.

It was like a scene in a waxworks. Or like a

picture painted in vivid oils. No one was moving. No one dared to move. Guthrie's men stood paralysed on the board-walk, not a limb twitching. One of them had been putting a plug of chewing tobacco in his mouth. It remained between frozen lips. Another had been pushing back his fedora. His hand stayed on the brim.

Catsfoot and Guthrie....

The tools of death were in their hands. A minute flexing of the index fingers would be death for both. Yes—for both. It could make no difference which of them fired first, for there would be a re-flex action by the other and the slugs would practically pass each other. Each of them knew that. So each was utterly still.

It was Guthrie who broke the agony of silence. His voice croaked because of the guns pressed into his throat as he said: "You'll have to drop your Colts, Catsfoot. You've got to think of the folks in the hotel."

"You've got just two minutes to release those people, Guthrie! Just two minutes, or I squeeze my triggers!"

"You'd die too!"

"I know it."

Guthrie licked his lips. He asked: "What about the prisoners? Do you want to kill 'em? I wasn't kiddin' when I said the sound of a shot would be an execution order."

"I never thought you were kidding, Guthrie.

But if you don't free those folks... I'll kill you and you'll kill me! That's the deal, Guthrie! I'm ready to die—*are you?*"

"You're crazy, Catsfoot! Mebbe you ain't scared, but you ain't the sort of man to be responsible for the end of a bunch of townsfolk, neither!"

Catsfoot pressed his "Dragoons"a fraction farther into Guthrie's neck. His eyes were ovals of blue steel.

"I figure their lives aren't worth much anyway, while you're holding them hostage," he said. "So you'd better make up your mind, Guthrie! Do you set them free? Or do we squeeze our triggers? You've got one minute left!"

Guthrie stole a couple of sidelong glances at his men. They could not help him. Even if they were to shoot Catsfoot—which they could do easily—those guns would explode into his throat. Even the slightest knock would be enough to jar Catsfoot's fingers back that tiny fraction necessary to release the hammers. And the same applied to Guthrie's gun.

At the other side of the street, Shaun listened to the thudding of his heart. He knew that Catsfoot was not bluffing. Catsfoot was not the type of man who bluffed. It was a desperate gamble. The stakes were his own life and the lives of several others. Yet it was the one chance of saving Gloryrise.

Guthrie was sweating.

Not ordinary sweat through the gathering heat of the day. It was cold, oozing oil of fear. It mingled with the bristles of his chin. It was shining on the bruised side of his head.

And he was asking: "What happens if I let those folks go free?"

"You give another order, Guthrie—you tell your outfit to ride out of town and stay out."

"Yep? Well that's an order I won't give."

"Okay, but we'll stay like this, gun against gun, till you change your mind, Guthrie. We'll see whose nerve breaks first."

But it seemed that Guthrie's nerve was already breaking. He said: "Okay, suppose I let the prisoners go and my outfit leaves town, what then? I'll be alone. D'you plan to kill me?"

Catsfoot gave a slight shake of his head.

"If I was going to kill you anyway, there'd be no sense in you making a deal. Once your mob's clear of Gloryrise, I'll let you ride after them. I don't like doing it, but I guess I'll have to."

Guthrie said: "Al—you heard it all. You know what to do."

Al eased forward.

"Y'want me...."

"I want you to get to the hotel and tell 'em to let the prisoners go."

Al hesitated, fury and confusion on his face. Then he ran towards the hotel.

And on the board-walk, all became motionless again. All became silent. The tall and slender figure of Catsfoot was bent slightly forward as he held his guns against Guthrie's throat. A slight breeze was ruffling his hair which flowed to his shoulders. Guthrie, not so tall but much broader, was in a semi-crouch as his "Frontier" thrust into Catsfoot's stomach.

Shaun saw Al disappear into the hotel. Then he heard footsteps behind him. It was Mrs. Hepple and she was no longer sobbing. She gave a bewildered look across the street.

"What's happenin', Shaun? Tell me!"

"It's goin' to be all right, Mrs. Hepple! Your brother's to be freed and so are all the others!"

She gasped her relief.

"But what's Catsfoot doing there with that— that Guthrie?"

Shaun tried to explain to her, but she did not fully understand. She was about to ask more questions when a handful of men came out of the hotel and stood blinking dazedly in the sunlight. Mrs. Hepple saw her brother. She gave a shrill shout and rushed towards him.

Other people were coming out of their homes or leaving the groups already in the street to run towards the freed prisoners. For the moment, the people of Gloryrise forgot the terror. And they forgot the man who was saving them from it.

Catsfoot could not turn his head to see, but he

knew from the babel of voices that he had won his part of the gamble.

He said to Guthrie: "Now you can order your outfit out of town."

"You're sure you won't murder me when they've gone."

"I've given my word."

"I figure I can rely on it," Guthrie said. Then he raised his voice and said to his men: "Y'all know the set-up. All of you get your hosses and ride north. I'll be followin' you."

There was an uncertain murmuring from the outfit. But slowly they began to move towards the town stables.

They did not move far.

Al stopped them. Al had returned from the hotel with three men who had been guarding the prisoners. His thin, rat-like face had been puckered in thought. But now it wore an evil smile.

"Not so fast," Al said. "I've got somethin' to say."

Without moving his head, Guthrie glanced at Al. He shouted hoarsely: "You gone crazy? I've given an order for you all to ride out and that goes for you, too, Al!"

Al mounted the board-walk. He halted within inches of the motionless figures of Catsfoot and Guthrie. He surveyed them with gloating satisfaction.

"I've been thinkin' mebbe you ain't the only one who can run this outfit," Al said to Guthrie.

Despite the guns on his throat, Guthrie gave something approaching a bellow.

"Now I know you're gone crazy! You and me are goin' to have a long talk about this when we're clear of the burgh!"

Casually, Al pulled his gun from its holster. With a finger through the trigger-guard, he twirled it.

"If we ride out of here we won't be able to come back so easy," he said, "'cause I figure this Catsfoot hombre'll have the place organised to beat us off. That means we're expected to give up a lot of soft pickings. Why? Just so's to save your hide, Guthrie! Well, I don't think your hide's worth it! If you and Catsfoot put a slug into each other, it needn't worry us none. We can stay here and mebbe I can boss the outfit!"

A tremor ran through Guthrie's huge body. For a second his gun quavered against Catsfoot's stomach as he fought the temptation to turn on Al. He conquered it. And he hissed out of one side of his mouth: "The outfit won't get along without me! I'm the fastest gun on earth!"

"Mebbe y'are," Al said. "Or mebbe this Catsfoot runs even with you. But it don't matter none, 'cause with both of you stone cold. *I'll* be the fastest gun. I'm nice and smart with a Colt *and* a sleeve-Derringer and I get good ideas.

Like this idea. So I figure the outfit'll be ready to take orders from me. Specially when it means we'll be able to stay on in this burgh for a while longer."

As he finished, Al turned to look at the others for approval. Some were nodding. But not all of them. Some were staring at each other doubtfully.

But their doubts were a detail. Shaun realised the ghastly truth that the foundation of Catsfoot's temporary power over the outfit was crumbling. It rested entirely on Guthrie's authority. On the assumption that Guthrie's life was so valuable too them that they would obey any order so as to preserve it. But Guthrie's leadership was being challenged by Al. And some, at least, were ready to follow Al because they wished to stay in Gloryrise.

Al tried to rally the doubters.

"Guthrie's washed up," he shouted. "He ain't so smart, or he wouldn't be stuck there with a couple of Colts in his neck! Mebbe they're scared to fire the first shot, so how say if I fix one of 'em...."

Al ceased twirling his gun. He levelled it between Catsfoot and Guthrie. Then he added: "I only need to give 'em a bit of a jerk and they'll put slugs into each other!"

There was a sudden movement among the men.

One of them shouted: "Go right ahead, Al. I'm with you!"

But another yelled: "You ain't makin' y'self boss, Al. You ain't got what it takes!"

There was a medley of harsh and furious accents, of accusation and counter-accusation.

"Al's our man! We ain't quittin' this burgh just to save Guthrie's skin…!"

"Guthrie's worth savin'—he's always led us okay…!"

"Use some sense! If we do like Al says we'll go on livin' soft…!"

"Yep, and mebbe we won't live so long…!"

It was chaos. And in the midst of it, no one noticed the group of four aged Apache traders. They rode into the main street from the southern trail. Baskets and blankets were slung over their ponies. They reined in and watched the scene, faces expressionless.

Now most of the outfit had drawn their guns. But they were hesitant, uncertain of what to do with them.

Then Catsfoot moved.

Catsfoot was counting on the fact that Guthrie's attention was divided, that an act which would have been fatal a minute earlier might just be possible now. He pivoted on his right heel and swung round. He swung away from the gun which was pressed into his stomach.

Guthrie squeezed his trigger.

He squeezed it a fraction late. The slug which was intended for Catsfoot screeched through empty air. It whined over the heads of the men who seethed just below the board-walk.

Then it found a mark. An unintended mark. The slug buried itself in the body of one of the Apaches.

The redskin's jaw fell slack. He swayed from side to side as though being tugged by a swirling wind. Then, without uttering a sound, he dropped backwards from his pony and lay twitching in the dust.

The shouting ceased. Everyone was gazing at the brown figure on the ground.

The three other Apaches sprang from their ponies and knelt beside him. A moment later Catsfoot, all else forgotten, was with them. So was Shaun. The bullet seemed to have travelled between the Indian's upper ribs. He was still alive—but only just.

Now everyone in the town was gathering round while the Apaches tore a length of blanket to make a bandage. Then, very carefully, they lifted the unconscious brave across a pony and secured him there with a girth rope between hands and feet.

The Apaches were about to leave Gloryrise when their leader spoke. He was the oldest of them. Wrinkles were carved into his lean face. Controlled fury showed in his eyes.

"We came in peace to trade with you," he said, "and you greet us with gunfire. For that you shall pay."

"It was an accident," Catsfoot said. "We're all sorry and..."

"Your sorrow will not be enough. The laws of my people call for justice."

"What sort of justice?"

The old Apache held up a forefinger as he replied: "You will send one white man to our camp before sundown. Just one of your number is all that we want. If our brave lives, the paleface will be returned to you and he will not be harmed. But if our brave should die, then the paleface will die, too."

There was a taut silence as the terms were uttered.

Then Catsfoot said: "Why don't you leave the brave here? There's a doctor around and he'd look after him."

"We do not trust your medicine. Remember —send one of your people to us before the sun sets."

Catsfoot asked: "If we refuse?"

"Hear me well, white people. If you refuse, we shall ride down on this place with ten times a hundred braves, all of them young and strong, as I am old and weak. We will burn this town till there is nothing left even for the carrion birds to eat. And we will take the scalps of every man, woman and child. I have spoken...."

CHAPTER FIVE

THE SACRIFICE

THE crowd parted to let the Apaches go. They left proudly, still with their simple trading goods. And with an unconscious figure dangling over the back of one of their ponies.

Fear-filled people watched them disappear round the bend of the main street.

Then most of the crowd drifted quietly away. When they talked, it was in undertones, as though scared of drawing attention to themselves. Some moved towards the saloon. Others to their homes.

But Guthrie's outfit remained in the street.

They grouped round Guthrie, looking anxiously at him, awaiting orders. He was again their un-challenged leader. Those who had remained loyal to him were congratulating themselves on their good sense. Those who had rebelled were hoping that it would be forgotten.

All except Al.

Al stood on the outer edge of the group. His face was strained, his hands were opening and closing nervously. The others tried to keep away from him. They all knew that Guthrie might forgive the others. But he would never forgive

Al. Sometime, somewhere, the score would be settled....

"What are we goin' to do, Guthrie?" a half-breed asked.

"We'll do like I said before—get out of here. I don't aim to be in this burgh when the Apaches arrive."

Now there was no opposition. For the second time within minutes the outfit began to move towards the stables. And for a second time they were stopped. It was Catsfoot who did it.

Catsfoot was standing a few paces away from the outfit, Shaun at his side.

"You seem to be forgetting something, Guthrie," Catsfoot said.

Guthrie gave him a quick, stealthy glance.

"Now what are you beefin' about, Catsfoot? You wanted us out of here, didn't you? We're goin', ain't we? You oughta be a real happy man."

"You seem to have forgotten it was your slug that hit that Apache."

"Sure it was. But I wouldn't have fired it if you hadn't tried to pull a smart move. I didn't want to shoot him and you know it."

Catsfoot nodded. He said slowly: "That's right—I'm not holding you responsible."

"That's nice to know, but it don't worry me one way or the other. I can still fix you any time I want and if you start talkin' too clever I'll want to right now!"

Catsfoot ignored the threat. He said: "Some-one's got to go out to the Apache camp. He won't come back if that Indian dies, but it's a chance someone's got to take if the town's to be saved from massacre."

Guthrie snorted contempt.

"That ain't my worry. It ain't my town. Anyway, if you're so durned anxious about it, why don't you go y'self?"

"Mebbe I will," Catsfoot said.

Guthrie raised heavy eyebrows.

"That's brave talk, Catsfoot! If you go out to the camp, I'll hope real hard that the Apache dies!"

"I only said *mebbe* I'll go. I figure it ought to be between you and me, Guthrie."

"Y'do, uh! Well I ain't playin' that kinda game—so that leaves you on your own."

"I was going to suggest flipping a silver dollar to decide on which of us," Catsfoot said, "but I guess it'd be wasting breath."

"It sure would be wastin' breath! Me and m'outfit are ridin' right out of here."

"I thought you'd say that, but I had to try you out. You're real yellow, ain't you, Guthrie! You don't mind about a whole town being mur-dered so long as you're okay!"

Guthrie pushed through the group of men, head jutting forward, huge shoulders flexing.

"No man calls me yellow!"

"I'm calling you yellow, Guthrie ... do you feel like going for your gun?"

It was a cold, calculated challenge. One, it seemed, which could not be ignored. Shaun waited for Guthrie to accept it. The outfit waited, too. Waited for the grotesquely fast movements of arms and wrists, for the sickening and reverberating explosions which would decide for ever which was the faster gun.

They did not come. Guthrie's gun hand quivered very slightly. But that was all.

And he said: "This ain't the time, Catsfoot. There ain't no sense in me givin' you a quick end if the Apaches are goin' to fix you with a long, painful one! But if the Apaches don't get you, I will! That's a promise, Catsfoot!"

He turned and strode towards the stables, the rest following.

Catsfoot stood quite still, watching them go.

And Shaun, at his side, knew that the almost incredible had happened. Guthrie was scared to draw on Catsfoot!

Perhaps it was instinct which told him that in Catsfoot there was the one man in the new territories who was at least as fast. Maybe even faster. It was no mere bravado which had prompted Catsfoot to make that challenge. It had been a deliberate attempt to humiliate Guthrie, to sow seeds of doubt about his mastery as a gunfighter. And it had succeeded.

Suddenly Shaun felt a hot surge of pride in his friendship with Catsfoot. Practically alone and un-aided, this tall and kindly man in buckskins had shaken a rule of terror. He had not destroyed it. Not even seriously weakened it. But he had achieved what no one else had been able to do—he had made a start. He had shown Gloryrise that Guthrie was not invincible. The story would spread, and other places in Arizona would take heart, too.

Shaun heard a fading thud of hooves. Guthrie's outfit were leaving town. But they were not going as they had arrived. There was no arrogance now. They were spurring their horses to a gallop, anxious to get away from the threat of the Apaches' vengeance.

The Apaches' vengeance....

If the town was to be spared, one man would have to stake his life on the chance of the wounded brave recovering. That man might be held in the camp for days or even weeks before knowing whether he was to be set free—or to suffer a ghastly death. Catsfoot had said that the choice was between himself and Guthrie. But Guthrie had fled. The idea of Catsfoot going out there filled Shaun with horror.

But now the townsfolk were gathering round Catsfoot.

In the last few minutes they had changed, those peaceful people of Gloryrise. They were taut under new danger. But they were ready to face it.

Their heads were high. They had found a leader.

Sam Timberley, who kept the looted merchantile store, said: "We were all watchin' when you challenged Guthrie just now and I guess none of us expected to see him duck a gunfight. We've gotta thank you, Catsfoot. I figure we'll have no more trouble from that outfit."

Catsfoot shook his head.

"I wouldn't count on that. Guthrie isn't finished—not by a long way and he could be meaner than ever after this. So before I leave you, I want you to organise a vigilante squad in case he comes back."

Timberley shouted: "You leavin' us, Catsfoot! You can't do that! Anyway, you're our new marshal!"

There was a roar of agreement. Catsfoot put up a hand for silence.

"Someone's got to go out to that Apache camp, "he said. "It's going to be me."

There were more shouts, this time of protest.

"You ain't doin' nothin' of the sort...!"

"That redskin hasn't much chance of livin', so it could be sure death for you...!"

"You've done plenty for us, Catsfoot, but you ain't doin' this...!"

"Anyway, we need you with us...!"

Catsfoot had to raise his voice above the tumult.

He said: "Someone's got to go. If I don't, who will?"

The question brought an abrupt silence. The people were faced with stark reality.

Then a plainsman said doubtfully: "Mebbe we can beat them Apaches off if they attack us."

"They *will* attack unless one of us surrenders to them before sunset," Catsfoot said. "To them it's only justice and I'm not saying they're not right."

"But Catsfoot, with you in charge we could give 'em a warm time."

"Yep, they'd suffer heavy casualties. But it'd need a couple of squadrons of cavalry to keep a thousand Apaches out of this town. And remember this—they weren't kidding when they said they'd scalp every man, woman and child. The Apaches aren't particular who they kill when they've tasted blood."

A man elbowed through the crowd. He stopped opposite Catsfoot and said: "I'll go. I *want* to go!"

Shaun recognised him with a dull shock. It was Matthew, his father's surviving deputy. The younger man whose nerve had broken when the outfit rode into Gloryrise. But there was no trace of fear about him now. He was composed and steady as he met Catsfoot's inquiring stare.

"You've sure got me puzzled," Catsfoot said.

"No one but a crazy man would *want* to go to the Apaches."

"I ain't crazy, but it's still the way I feel. Yesterday, when Guthrie came into town, I stood alongside Herb Brent and another deputy. Two of us did our duty and one of us died. But me? I snivelled and whined to keep my skin whole. I let down all the folks here, I let down Herb Brent, and what was worst of all, I let m'self down. Since then I've done a lot of thinkin'. I've decided it's better for a man to die on his feet than live on his knees. That's why I want to give m'self to the Apaches. It's my chance to win back a bit of self-respect."

Catsfoot's face was expressionless as he asked: "You're Matthew, aren't you? Shaun told me about you."

"He wouldn't tell you anything to m'credit and I don't blame him. Right now, I ain't worth a cent as a man. But I aim to do something to change that."

Catsfoot smiled. He gripped Matthew's hand.

"You're worth a lot as a man," he said. "You're worth as much as me or anyone else here."

Matthew looked confused and puzzled.

"I guess you don't understand. I've acted real yellow."

"I do understand, Matthew. Yesterday your nerve gave way because there was nothing you could do to help Herb Brent. That kind of thing can happen to any man and you've got to forget it. You're still a deputy, aren't you?"

"Yep, I guess so."

"That puts you under my orders, doesn't it?"

"I figure it does, you bein' temporary marshal."

"Okay—you're to take charge here while I give myself to the Apaches."

Matthew raised an indignant fist.

"But I want to go! I will go!"

Catsfoot told him: "I was partly responsible for that redskin being hit, so I'll have to face it out myself. No one else is going to do it for me and there'll be no more argument about it. Right now, I'm going to get some rest and I guess Shaun needs it, too. I'll leave for the Apaches' camp this afternoon…."

Catsfoot slept in the chair behind the desk in the marshal's office. His long legs stretched out, gun belt on the floor, he seemed completely untroubled.

But Shaun, on his own bunk in the tiny room above, could only doze fitfully. He was weary, but real sleep would not come. Catsfoot was always on his mind. He was tormented by visions of what the Apaches would do to him if that redskin died. There was not the slightest doubt that the Apaches would keep their word in every way. They were a ruthless race and they were noted in warfare for their cunning rather than bravery, being natural tacticians. But they were also honourable within strict limits. A threat or a promise would be carried out, so long as it did not cause any hardship to them. If the wounded brave recovered, Catsfoot would certainly be unharmed. But if the brave died....

Shaun had heard people speak of the agonies the Apaches inflicted on white prisoners before slaying them. He sweated and almost moaned as he thought of them.

Then a noise disturbed his misery.

It was the chatter of urgent voices in the main street.

At first, it did not make any deep impression on him. The sound reached him clearly enough through the open window of his room. But he only wondered idly why people were gathering outside during the heat of the early afternoon. But the voices became louder and more confused, as if the crowd were becoming bigger. Fully awake now, Shaun got off his bunk and looked through the window.

It was happening almost directly below him.

An Apache was sitting erect on a glistening pony. But this was no old Indian trader. He was a young brave of the Mescalero sect, lean and as strong as a whip. His copper face was made hideous with purple war dye, squeezed from the roots of cactii. In his right hand he held aloft a seven-foot lance. He was ignoring the babbling of the crowd. His eyes were fixed on the door of the office, as if waiting for someone to emerge.

And at that moment Shaun saw Catsfoot come out.

Shaun did not hesitate any longer. He clattered down the short and narrow staircase. He emerged on the board-walk just as Catsfoot was beginning to speak.

"You want me?" Catsfoot was asking the Apache.

The Apache's eyes were heavy with hate.

"I bring a message from my people to yours."

"I'm the marshal of this town now. I'll hear it in the office."

The Apache shook his head.

"It will be uttered so all can hear."

"All right, if that's the way you want it."

"Our brother who came in peace to this place is no longer among us."

"You mean…"

"He died before he reached our camp. One of your number must come to us before sundown to die also. We care not who it is, but his death is now certain. If no one comes to us as a sacrifice, the whole of this town shall perish. That is my message."

He raised the lance high, then thrust it into the ground. It was still quivering there as he galloped away.

There are times when men cannot speak because they have too much to say. This was one of them. Everyone was silent, their minds teeming with fears and questions which were too muddled to be put into words.

Shaun stared at the strained faces, all of them watching Catsfoot. Watching half in hope, half in shame.

Catsfoot broke the uneasy quiet. He gave his slow smile and asked: "How long does it take to reach the camp from here?"

Shaun croaked: "About… about an hour."

"I guess I'd better get started soon. No sense in waiting around."

Shaun could not control himself any longer. He rushed at Catsfoot and gripped him round the waist. Tears were standing out in his eyes.

"You can't do this, Catsfoot! We won't let you! It's … it's just certain death now… certain death. You … you came into our town to help us and we ain't goin' to let you be tortured to death by the Apaches!"

There was a rumble of agreement.

A voice said: "We'll draw lots for who goes out there! Every able man in Gloryrise takes his chance—I figure that's fair."

There was a moment of hesitation, as if each person was trying to calculate the chances against being the victim. Then came a shout of agreement.

But Catsfoot said: "I haven't changed my mind. No one's going except me. I've already given you one reason, now I'll give another—every man in this burgh must have a family. I haven't got anyone. No one's going to weep too much about me."

But Shaun was weeping. He pressed his head into Catsfoot's buckskins so that no one would see. And he sobbed: "That ain't true! We need you ... everyone in Arizona needs you and men like you!"

Catsfoot put a hand under Shaun's chin and raised his head. He smiled down at him.

"Hey, Shaun—it isn't like you to break down. It doesn't make it any easier for me, when you act like that. Mebbe some folks are worth weeping over, but I'm not one of them. There's nothing special about me. I'm just an ordinary trail scout who can use his guns fast, but I never was a hero. This is my duty, and I figure every man has to do that ... now give me a grin, eh?"

Shaun wiped his eyes on his sleeve. He stared dazedly at the ground, his mind almost numb.

Then he felt people pushing against him. And a sudden pressure of bodies.

It was the people of Gloryrise.

They were packing tight round Catsfoot. So tight that he could scarcely move a limb. And they were doing it silently. No one had suggested it. It was instinctive among all of them.

Catsfoot asked: "What's this? You folks aiming to suffocate me?"

Sam Timberley, who was pressing against Catsfoot's right arm, gave the answer. He said: "You're not leavin' here, Catsfoot. You can't fight all of us and all of us have decided on this. We'll keep you in this town if we have to lock you in your own jail!"

"Don't talk crazy! I've got…"

"You've gotta give a pledge to stay right here! The rest of us'll draw lots to decide who's to be killed by the Apaches."

"I won't give any pledge! Now listen…."

But they did not listen. Several pairs of hands gripped his arms. He struggled and managed to tear himself free. But only for the barest moment. More hands clutched at him. Catsfoot twisted like a snake. But against such numbers and without room to manœuvre he was as helpless as a man in quicksands. A Goliath could not have escaped.

He was half carried and half pushed on to the board-walk, then into the office.

Slowly the swaying mass of people, Catsfoot in the centre, reached the small side door which opened into the jail. Someone found the keys and the iron-barred gate of the tiny cell was unlocked. Catsfoot was still struggling as he was pushed into it. Then the gate was locked.

The front of the crowd was pushing against the bars, breathing hard and smiling at him.

Sam Timberley said: "We're sorry to have to do this, Catsfoot, but it's the way we feel. I figure

you must be the first man to be locked in jail
'cause folks like him! And you the new marshal,
too!"

There was a faint, good-humoured laugh from
some of them. But Catsfoot did not join in. He
stared miserably through the bars.

"I know you mean well," he said, "but you're
making a big mistake."

"It ain't no mistake. You'll stay right here till
we've drawn lots and one of us is on his way to the
Apaches. Now I guess we'll have to leave you here
for a while, but y'can keep y'guns, seein' we don't
have no real quarrel."

Timberley dropped the jail keys in his pocket.
Gradually the crowd moved out of the building
until only Shaun was left with Catsfoot.

Catsfoot said to him: "You've got to let me
out of here. Are there any spare keys?"

Shaun shook his head.

"No, and I wouldn't let you out anyway."

"So you feel like the rest of them?"

"I sure do. None of us wants to see you put
to a slow death."

Catsfoot shrugged and went to the grilled window
at the back of the cell. He stared out over the
fringes of the town to the vast plains, shimmering
green and purple with sagebrush and soapweed.

But suddenly he spun round. So did Shaun.

It was a thin, dry gasp that they heard. Then a
meaningless shout. Mrs. Hepple burst into the

jail block and she was clutching a scrap of paper.
She waved it frantically above her head. And
she looked desperately at Shaun.

"It's... it's your pop!" she gasped.

"Pop! Has he taken a turn for worse...?"
And Shaun started to run for the door. But she
stopped him.

"He's gone!"

"Gone...!"

Shaun repeated the word unbelievingly.

"It's all here, in this note he left on his bunk.
He..."

Shaun snatched it from her. In a breaking voice,
he read aloud the scrawled words.

"*You've got to be calm about this, Son,*" the
message said. "*I heard what happened about them
Apaches. I figure I've got back enough of my strength
to saddle a horse and go out to the camp myself.
Seeing I'm wounded bad already, it ain't likely
I'll suffer for long at their hands. In fact, I reckon
I'll die quick when the redskins start on me and that's
more than can be said for anyone else. So don't worry
too much. You just stick around with Catsfoot and
do like he says. I've money in the bank at Tucson
and I've a lawyer there who'll see you don't go short
of nothing. Love from your Pop.*"

Shaun stared incredulously at Mrs. Hepple.
Then he looked again at the words.

"Pop couldn't do it," he whispered. "He's
too ill to do it!"

Mrs. Hepple said helplessly: "But he has done it. Herb always was a tough man and it's like he says—he was gettin' his strength back fast."

Catsfoot spoke. In hard, precise tones he said: "Stand back against the far wall, both of you."

He had his guns out.

Shaun blinked at him and asked: "What's... what's the idea?"

"Your father can't have got far and I'm going to try to bring him back. But first I've got to get out of here. That means I'll have to shoot this lock out."

"But mebbe Mister Timberley will let you free as soon as he knows about pop."

"I can't waste time waiting for that," Catsfoot said. "Now keep close to the wall—the slug's liable to bounce around."

The lock was of the simple single-tumbler type. But—as with all locks—a bullet in the wrong place would merely twist and jam the mechanism so that it would be impossible to get out without dismantling the entire gate. There was only one sure way of destroying it with a bullet. The secret lay in the square hinge-pin. This was embedded in a groove at the top of the bolt, preventing it moving except when the key was turned. Shatter that pin and the bolt could be pushed back under finger pressure. But it was concealed and protected by heavy iron casing. The difficulty was to smash it without warping the rest of the mechanism. It was a matter of knowing exactly where to place the bullet. Catsfoot knew where....

He braced himself against the bars. Carefully, he placed one of his Colt "Dragoons" at an angle of sixty degrees against the top of the casing. Then he drew it back half an inch.

And he squeezed the trigger.

In that confined space, the explosion was like that of a cannon. It vibrated the eardrums and made the head sing.

The casing bulged, as if made of rubber. Sparks splattered out of it.

On the wall opposite, Shaun saw a white streak suddenly appear as the distorted bullet shaved across the wood before burying itself in a corner near the floor.

Catsfoot was pushing a forefinger against the visible section of the bolt. With the hinge-pin gone, it slid back. He wrenched open the gate. And he seemed to have forgotten the existence of Shaun and Mrs. Hepple. Forgotten everything except that he must get out of the building fast. Two of his long, gliding steps took him into the adjacent office. Timberley was coming in the outer door. Several other townsfolk were with him, including Matthew.

"Hey," Timberley said, "we let y'keep y'guns, but we didn't reckon you'd try to shoot your way out! It won't do you no good, Catsfoot. We ain't finished drawin' lots yet so you'll..."

"You won't need to draw lots," Catsfoot rapped. "Herb Brent's gone!"

Timberley's jaw fell slack. Then he tried to frame a bewildered question. But Catsfoot had pushed past. No one tried to stop him as he strode on to the board-walk. Two horses were tethered to a nearby hitching-rail. He vaulted over the rail and into the saddle of one of them. He was leaning forward to untie the rein when Shaun came running up.

Shaun gasped: "I've just looked in our stable ... Pop's got away all right!"

"Do you know the trail he'd take to the Apaches' camp?"

"Sure—it's due north. I'll come with you!"

"You'll stay right here!"

"I'm comin', Catsfoot, and you ain't stoppin' me!"

They could not argue. There was no time for that. And Shaun did not give the opportunity, for he had already jumped into the saddle of the other horse.

He was close behind Catsfoot when, in a spray of dust, they galloped out of Gloryrise.

Fifteen minutes later they sighted Herb Brent.

They saw him when they topped a rise of rock-strewn ground. He was less than half a mile ahead and approaching a line of hills which marked the boundary of the Apaches' reservation.

Brent was not upright in the saddle. He was slumped over the neck of his horse and it seemed that his arms were clasped round it. The uncontrolled animal was moving at a slow, veering trot.

Shaun shouted: "He'll collapse any time!"

"We'll be with him in a couple of minutes, Shaun!"

But at that moment Brent's horse came to a slithering halt.

From behind the hills an Apache war party had appeared. They were lashing their ponies towards Brent and fanning out to form a circle round him.

CHAPTER SIX

PLEDGE OF THE APACHES

IT WAS not a race. Not a bid to reach Brent first. From their first appearance, the Apaches were much nearer to him. Within moments their circle had tightened until it had engulfed Brent. Then they dismounted and stood round him, waiting calmly for the arrival of Catsfoot and Shaun.

Shaun leapt from the saddle as he reined in. Vaguely, he was aware of the hideously painted faces which looked blankly at him. Faintly, the acrid smell of Apache bodies was in his nostrils. But he knew only that he must reach his father. He tried to rush towards him, but two brown hands gripped him and held him secure.

Shaun was near to hysteria. He writhed and kicked, but it was useless. He shouted: "That's m'pop and he's wounded bad!" But the Apaches did not seem to understand. They did not speak, they did not show any emotion. There were more than a dozen of them in that war party and they were like the phantom figures of a nightmare.

Then Shaun felt strong fingers take hold of his hair. His head was jerked back, so that he was looking up into the face of one of the braves.

But this was no ordinary Apache. Even amid his desperation, Shaun knew that.

This was an exceptionally tall Apache—almost as tall as Catsfoot. He was older than most of the others, but still at his physical best. The leather band round his head was etched with gold dust, so that it glittered. But it was his features which were compelling. They were gaunt and they were typically ruthless. Yet, beneath the streaks of disfiguring dye, a strange nobility showed, too. The sort of inherent dignity which can be seen in a thoroughbred animal. And when he spoke, his English was fluent and correct. It had none of the stilted uncertainty which was usual among Apaches trying to speak a strange tongue.

He asked Shaun: "What is this man to you that you should seek him so?"

"He's m'pop ... I mean my father."

The Apaches turned to look at the limp figure of Herb Brent, still clinging to his horse.

"He cannot say much, but he has told us he has come to offer his life. That is well, but before he dies you may speak with him."

He released his grip on Shaun's hair. Shaun rushed to his father's side.

Herb Brent was little more than semi-conscious. His body was arched over the saddle pommel. His head rested on the horse's mane, his arms were still gripping its neck. Shaun saw that his skin had an ugly yellowish pallor. The bandages across his chest were visible under his jacket and they were stained with new blood—he had probably reopened the wound while struggling to put on that jacket.

Brent turned his face very slightly. The simple movement was obviously a painful effort.

"You shouldn't have done this, Shaun," he whispered.

Suddenly Catsfoot was at Shaun's side. Very gently and quite easily, Catsfoot lifted Brent from the horse's back and laid him on the ground. There he lifted an edge of the bandage and looked at the wound.

"You've done yourself a lot of no good," Catsfoot told him. "But you'll be okay if we can get you back to Gloryrise."

Brent shook his head feebly.

"It's too late to talk like that. The Apaches want a life and it's goin' to be mine."

Catsfoot did not answer. He straightened up and turned towards the tall Apache.

"I offer my life in his place," he said. "I guess there's no reason for you to refuse."

The Apache folded his arms across his chest.

"If you wish it so," he said simply. "One white man is all we want and it does not matter who he is—but why do you want to die?"

"I don't want to die, but I'd rather it's me than him."

"Is he your brother?"

"Not my brother exactly, but he's my friend," Catsfoot said. "He isn't responsible for the killing of one of your braves, but in a way I was. It was an accident and it wasn't my gun, but I was partly the cause of it happening."

The Apache gazed levelly at Catsfoot and Catsfoot gazed back. They were standing within inches of each other. A long and uneasy silence settled on the war party. It was broken by the Apache.

"You meet the challenge of my eyes," he said, "and it is good. How call you?"

"The name's Catsfoot."

"I have heard that name and it is said you have never sought trouble with my people. You are speaking with Cochise."

Cochise...!

Shaun blinked as he heard the name. It was a legend in Arizona. Cochise was leader of the Chirichua Apaches, but he was also the accepted chief of many other sects, including the Mescaleroes. It was said that Cochise enjoyed slaying whites more than anything else, that there was no limit to his cruelty and his cunning.

And yet those who were not often wrong—those who sought the full facts before passing judgment—hinted that there was a time when he had sincerely sought friendship with the whites. They said that he had been transformed into a relentless enemy only because of the blundering stupidity years before of a young cavalry officer newly passed out of West Point. That officer—a Lieutenant George N. Bascom—had asked to see Cochise under a flag of truce to discuss the abduction of a half-breed boy named Mickey Free. Lieutenant Bascom, it was said, had accused Cochise of taking the boy. But Cochise had shown that he was completely unaware of the crime. It was the work of *bronco* Redskins, he had said. And he had explained that *broncos* were Indians not belonging to any tribe. He offered to track down the culprits and hand them over to the Lieutenant for justice. But Lieutenant Bascom had been too foolish and inexperienced to realise that Cochise was speaking the truth. Instead, he arrested the Apache and some of his men, in defiance of the flag of truce. And he announced that he would hold them as hostages against the boy's return. Cochise escaped, although wounded while doing so. And from that moment a friend of the white people turned into a remorseless foe.

Now he was feared over a vast area from Arizona's Gila River to deep into Mexico. Thousands of soldiers were seeking him, but had never been able to find him. He struck with the speed of lightning, then vanished into mountain strongholds. He placed a stranglehold on stagecoach routes and on wagon trains.*

*Cochise finally made peace with the whites in September, 1871, after the intervention of President Grant. He died years later - of old age.

All that and much more Shaun recalled as he looked in wonder at the Apache.

But Catsfoot did not show any emotion. He said: "I thought it was you, Cochise. But you're not usually in this part of Arizona."

"We were riding for the Mimbres River when a signal came to us that one of our people had been slain by the whites."

"So you took over? It was you who sent the demand for a life in return?"

Cochise nodded.

"I was told that the little town had never before sought to harm the Apaches. It was only because of that I decided to give it a chance."

Catsfoot said: "Then you needn't worry about attacking Gloryrise. You've got a life to destroy— mine."

Cochise was silent again, as though thinking. Then he said: "You speak of an accident and of the gun of another. Speak to me of it and I will listen."

"It's not a pretty story, Cochise, and I don't think it'll interest you."

"Tell it, I say."

In dry sentences Catsfoot described the events leading to the killing of the old Apache trader.

When he had finished, Cochise said: "You do ask mercy of me?"

"I don't. I know the law of your people and I'm ready to pay."

Cochise touched his own face. Then he slowly extended the hand until the tips of his fingers touched Catsfoot's cheeks.

"Our skins are not the same," he said. "But beneath our skins there is no difference between us. We are both men, you and I. Now hear me—you speak of the dog Guthrie. I charge you to find him and to bring him to me alive!"

"Bring him to you ! But I told you, Guthrie no more intended that particular killing than I did. Guthrie deserves to die many times over, but I figure it'd be wrong just to hand him to you…."

"I did not say that we would slay Guthrie. I charged you to bring him here—that is all. If you do that, the town will be preserved. If you fail, I will give the order for massacre. That is my new offer to you and I will not change it."

Catsfoot pushed back his fedora. Now he was puzzled and he was showing the fact.

"But if you're not going to kill Guthrie, does that mean you still want my life?"

"That you will know if you bring Guthrie to this place."

Catsfoot shrugged. Then he said: "Mebbe I won't be able to find him. And even if I do, he's got all his men with him. It seems you're asking the impossible, Cochise."

"To men such as we, all is possible. Many times have I tried to ambush wagon trains which

Brent lay on a litter slung between the Apaches' ponies.

you, Catsfoot, have been leading. But never have I been able to find them. It is well said that you are the greatest of the white scouts, so I do not ask too much of you."

"How long have I got?"

"We will wait at this place for you till this hour to-morrow. If you are not here with Guthrie by then, we shall descend upon Gloryrise."

"But if I can't bring Guthrie, surely you'll leave the town alone if I return alone!"

"If you return alone you will be at my side to watch the end of Gloryrise."

And that was all Cochise would say. He would give no further hint of the strange workings of his mind.

An hour later, when the sinking sun was glowing red over the main street, Shaun, Brent, and two Apaches entered Gloryrise. A plaited grass litter had been slung between the Apaches' ponies and Brent lay on it. He was sleeping and some of the pallor had gone from his face.

The townsfolk stared at the group in silent astonishment. Then they clustered round Shaun, asking anxious questions.

Shaun answered them as best he could. And just before he followed his father into the office he said in a dazed way: "Catsfoot's gone after Guthrie alone … alone against more than twenty men."

Matthew the deputy said: "We'd have helped him! We'd have got up a posse."

"He wouldn't wait for a posse. He said there was no time. And he wouldn't even take me with him. He just asked me to tell you all that if he failed to bring back Guthrie he'd return to this town to die with us…."

CHAPTER SEVEN

THE BORDER TRAIL

GUTHRIE raised his canteen of stew to his mouth and drained it. Then he wiped his mouth with the back of a hand and stretched out his legs.

"That wasn't bad chuck," he said, "and it was all the nicer for bein' a gift from Gloryrise."

The outfit grinned. They had halted in a clearing amid a thick cluster of cottonwood trees. The fire of scrub bathed them all in a cheerful glow. The moon gave a thin light through the leaves.

"I figure we'll cross into Mexico in the mornin'," Guthrie added.

Someone asked: "Why are we headin' for Mexico?"

"Why? 'Cause there's a place called Puerto Penasco in Mexico. It's not a hundred miles from where we are now and it's on the Gulf of California."

"Penasco? I ain't never heard of it. What's so special about that place, Guthrie?"

"Nothin' special, except the folks there live nice and fat. I figure we can live fat, too—as their guests."

There was a gust of raw laughter. They all understood.

A man who had just lit a long cheroot said: "I'd sure like to know what happened to Gloryrise. Mebbe that burgh ain't there no more."

"I figure it'll be okay," Guthrie said. "That slob Catsfoot was crazy enough to offer himself up to the Apaches to save the place. He'd do anything just so he could look big."

An uneasy silence fell on the ring of men round the fire at the mention of Catsfoot. All of them stared into the crackling flames. All of them avoided Guthrie's eye.

Guthrie looked carefully at them. Looked at each man in turn. Suddenly he sprang up. He put both hands on his thick waist and jutted his head forward.

"What's the matter?" he bellowed in a voice which echoed among the dark trees. "You all look kinda different when I mention Catsfoot? You think I'm scared of him, uh? Mebbe you figure I was too yellow to draw on him just before we left Gloryrise? Does anyone think that? If anyone's thinkin' that way, he has m'permission to speak up!"

No one spoke.

Guthrie moved round the fire. He made a complete circle of it. Then he kicked viciously at a red faggot. It careered towards some of the outfit. They had not rolled out of its path, but they did not dare to protest. Right now, Guthrie was extra dangerous. No one but a fool would try crossing words with him.

He glowered at the men, his face evil in the light of the flames. Then abruptly his animal eyes probed around—looking for one man.

"Where's Al?" he asked.

They all turned. All tried to locate Al.

Al was sitting well outside the circle. His back was propped against one of the smooth-barked trees and he was holding a mug of coffee. But he had forgotten about that coffee. It was motionless, a few inches from his thin lips.

"Why are you skulkin' there, Al?" Guthrie shouted.

Al did not answer. He was utterly still, as though frozen alive.

"Are y'scared of me, Al?"

Al moved now, but only very slightly. The mug began to shake with his hand and hot coffee slopped on to his knees. There was a whine in his voice as he said: "I guess we're all a bit scared of you, Guthrie." And he attempted to finish off with an admiring laugh. But it was no more than a whimpering snivel.

Guthrie's tones changed. They were soft and caressing as he said: "Come here, Al. Come close.... I wanta talk with you."

Al put the mug on the ground. His bony face was twitching. He remained seated.

"Didn't y'hear me, Al? I said for you to come here!"

Slowly Al got to his feet. He wavered, as if wondering whether to risk a dash into the dark shelter of the trees. Then he advanced towards Guthrie, a slack and sickly smile distorting his mouth.

His steps became slower and he stopped with a couple of paces between them.

"Come closer," Guthrie purred.

Al edged a reluctant half step.

"D'you still feel like takin' over this outfit?" Guthrie asked him.

Al's parody of a smile had gone. The flesh of his face hung slack. He was like a rabbit confronting a rattlesnake.

"I... I...."

His voice faded out as though he had been strangled.

"Speak up, Al! You ain't got anything to be scared about."

It was a smooth, apparently genuine assurance. Some of Al's terror vanished.

"I'm ... I'm sure glad to know that, Guthrie."

"Of course you are. But I can't understand why you were ever worried. You're a faster gun than me, ain't you, Al?"

Renewed fear enveloped Al. He shook his head violently.

"Nope! I ain't never claimed to be faster

than you, Guthrie! You're the fastest gun on earth!"

"That's nice to hear. Tell me, Al—d'you figure I'm faster than that Catsfoot?"

"I sure do! Catsfoot'd be just one more killin' for you!"

"That's the way I see it, too, Al. It's a big relief to me to know we agree about a big thing like that." Guthrie paused and ran his tongue over his lips. When he spoke again it was in another echoing shout. "So we'll get back to talkin' about you wantin' to run the outfit, Al!"

"I tell you, Guthrie, I don't want to run it! Honest, I don't."

"I seem to remember you had different ideas back in Gloryrise!"

"I was crazy, Guthrie! I didn't mean it! You see, I wanted to get..."

"Sure, Al, I understand. But I'm goin' to give you a chance to be the boss, Al. All you've gotta do is draw on me. If you draw fast enough, you'll be a big man."

"I don't wanta draw on you, Guthrie! I couldn't lick you!"

Guthrie nodded. It was almost an understanding nod.

"So you ain't ambitious any more, Al? Mebbe you'll tell me just how sorry you are, eh?"

"Y'know I'm sorry, Guthrie. There's only one boss of this outfit and it's you."

Guthrie said: "Keep still, Al. Don't move an inch...." He stretched out a hand. It lingered over the butt of Al's gun. It lifted the gun out of its holster. With a flick of the wrist Guthrie sent it into the foliage.

Al gazed perplexed at the empty holster. Then an expression which was on the outer fringe of fury quavered on his face.

"You can't do that, Guthrie!"

"I've done it."

"But you can't take a man's gun away—not in this territory! It's worse than killin' him out-right!"

Guthrie laughed as he said: "You don't count as a man any more, Al. From now on, you're just the dogie of this outfit. You'll rub down the horses, you'll polish the leathers, you'll clean our saddle boots and you'll cook the chuck. That'll be your work, Al. You won't need a gun—so I'll take that Derringer you keep up your sleeve, too."

Guthrie's hand streaked out and gripped Al's left forearm. He squeezed it and Al gave a whimpering groan. The shape of the tiny pistol showed clearly through the material of the jacket. With his other hand, Guthrie ripped the cloth. He snatched out the Derringer. It followed the Colt into the foliage.

When Guthrie stood back, Al was still groaning and he began rubbing his arm.

Guthrie bellowed: "You ain't worth a bullet,

Al—or I'd have given you one. But remember this, I'll never have m'eyes off you. You won't run out on me. You're goin' to stay with me and I'll make y'eat dirt. You'll never get away from me, Al. Remember that, when you wake up...."

Guthrie's left fist jabbed deep into the centre of Al's stomach. Al's head came down as though on a hinge. But only for a moment. Guthrie's other fist detonated across the angle of the jaw. Al's thin frame shook like a spar of wood. At the same time it jerked backwards and he somersaulted across the clearing. He rolled into the undergrowth and remained there, only his legs visible.

Al felt as if he were being dragged under deep water. He wanted to breathe, yet knew that he could not do so.

It was the weird agony of recovering from a knock-out blow.

But slowly his brain cleared. He did not move and did not want to move. It was better, he thought, to remain there with most of his body concealed from the outfit. His stomach was aching and there was a dull pain in his jaw. But he was suffering most from crushing humiliation. His guns had been taken from him! He was now the lackey of the outfit! The menial who cleaned the horses and served the chuck. Now Al knew the torment of hopeless hate. He wanted to fix

Guthrie. But he could not do so. If he tried to flee, Guthrie would follow as a cat follows a mouse....

Through the brush he could just see the glow of the camp fire. And he could hear occasional murmurs of talk. It seemed that the outfit were about to sleep. He decided that he would sleep, too. Sleep just where he was....

Something was pressing against his mouth. It was adding to the ache in his jaw. Something very strong. It was holding his whole head down, so that he could not raise his body and could not utter a sound.

Al was almost afraid to open his eyes. But he did open them—very slightly. A sweating face was close to his own. The face of a man in stained buckskins. That man was crouching over Al. And Al knew him.

"Listen to me," Catsfoot said in the softest of whispers. "If you want to get even with Guthrie, listen and don't make any sound! You ready to do that?"

Al managed to nod his head very slightly. The hand was taken from his mouth.

Catsfoot whispered again: "Don't try to double-cross me! If you do, you'll never double-cross anyone else! But if you work with me, I'll make you a free man! Free of Guthrie! Play it my way, and you'll be in no danger because my guns'll be covering you all the time. I won't let Guthrie touch you! That's my promise and this is what you've got to do…."

A faint rustle in the scrub. So faint that it all but mingled with the night breeze in the cotton-wood leaves. But Guthrie heard it as he dozed. It came from the place where Al had been sprawled. Guthrie looked towards that spot. But he could see little save deep shadows, for the fire was almost out and there was no longer much light from it.

At first Guthrie did not move. He remained as if still asleep. And he listened.

Another rustle. Then a heavier sound. It was certainly a foot being placed carefully on to the ground—but not carefully enough. It seemed to be making for the far side of the clearing, where the horses were tethered.

Guthrie rolled on to his stomach. He drew his knees under his chest then sprang upright in a single, silent bound. He did not even disturb a twig. It was a remarkable feat for such a heavily-built man.

Then he waited, ears straining.

He heard the unmistakeable clink of a bridle chain as the bit-iron was pushed into a horse's mouth. He heard the animal stamp. Someone else heard it, too. One of the outfit who had been sleeping next to Guthrie half rose. Guthrie gestured him to keep still and whispered: "It seems like Al doesn't like us no more. I figure that's him tryin' to move out. Leave him to me. I'm goin' to handle Al m'self...."

Carefully, Guthrie moved towards the horses. He stopped when their dim outlines came in sight. He saw one such outline detach itself from the rest and vanish among the trees. Guthrie sucked his lips with satisfaction. It was certain that Al would lead his animal until he was well clear of the camp. Anyway, the trees were too thick for riding in the dark. It would be easy enough to follow him. And to halt him at the right moment —the moment when Al was congratulating himself on getting clear away. Guthrie almost laughed. This was going to be good....

Guthrie quickened his pace. Even though it was obviously being led slowly, Al's horse was creating noise among the foliage. Once, when the moon showed through a gap in the tree tops, he glimpsed man and beast. They were about twenty yards in front, heading north—away from the border. Guthrie decided that the time had come to cut him off. He would have some fun with Al. Then he would fix him for good....

Guthrie moved off to his left. And he moved in a fast semi-circle, which would bring him in front of Al.

Somewhere close by, a coyote was howling.

Guthrie realised that he had not heard that howl when he was in the clearing. That showed he had moved a long way from the camp. He decided to get back as soon as he could. Maybe he wouldn't waste too much time on Al. It would be enough just to see the scare on him. Then to fix him....

Al felt as if he was floundering in a barrel of cold grease. Sweat was oozing from every part of his body, soaking his clothes and making them cling to him. One hand was pushed under his belt to keep it steady. The other was vibrating like a hair-spring as it guided the horse.

He wished he had not agreed to this. Guthrie was sure to be after him now. Somewhere in this blackness, Guthrie must be stalking him.

And Catsfoot?

Catsfoot was supposed to be stalking Guthrie.

Al thought: "M'skin depends on Catsfoot... mebbe I was crazy to listen to him...."

It was then that it happened.

The horse whinnied and tossed back its head, wrenching the leathers from Al's trembling grip.

A substantial shadow was standing only a yard in front.

And a voice was saying: "You plannin' to go any place special, Al?"

It was Guthrie's voice, lilting and horrible. Al felt the juices dry within him so that he became only a husk of a man.

He tried to remember what Catsfoot had said. Yes, Catsfoot had told him that when this moment

came he must *talk*! Talk to Guthrie about anything for at least a minute.

"I couldn't... couldn't sleep, Guthrie. There's
an ache in my face where y'slugged me and it's kept
me awake."

"Yep? So you figured on takin' a ride around,
eh? Just to settle your weary nerves, I guess."

"That's right," Al croaked. "I won't be goin'
far."

"You won't be goin' anywhere that'll interest
you, Al. I thought mebbe you'd try to run out on
me. Nobody does that to me, Al. First you
wanta take over the outfit, then you try to quit.
You ain't reliable."

Guthrie eased forward until he was only inches
from Al. In the faint moonlight it was now just
possible to make out his slab-like face.

"You don't understand, Guthrie! I wouldn't
run out on you! Honest I wouldn't!"

"That's not the way ... *ahh* ... !"

Guthrie ended with a choking gasp. He swayed.
Then it was as if his spine had dissolved. He
folded to the ground and lay there face down,
very still.

Catsfoot materialised out of the blackness. He
was holding one of his guns by the barrel. He
muttered: "I don't like having to slug any man
from the back, but there was no other way ... you
okay, Al?"

The tension over, Al was breathing fast and deep,

as if he had been running a long distance. He gasped: "Yep, I'm fine. Are you sure Guthrie's out cold?"

"He'll be unconscious for a few minutes. By the time he comes round he won't be able to make any trouble."

Catsfoot knelt beside the unconscious body. He removed Guthrie's neckcloth and tore it into halves. One section went into Guthrie's mouth. The other was used to lash his hands behind his back. Al watched, eyes straining through the dark.

Catsfoot made a careful check of the knots. Then he said: "When he comes round he'll be going on your horse, Al."

"My hoss! You can't take that! I've gotta get out of here too. What am I goin' to use?"

"You'll have to go back to the camp and get yourself another. It won't be difficult if you're quiet."

"I ain't doin' that! It could be dangerous."

"There's no danger if you're careful—but you'd better be on your way right now, Al. Daylight isn't so far off."

Al hesitated. Then he vanished into the darkness.

Catsfoot knelt again and peered at Guthrie. He was groaning. But presently the groans ceased. After a brief interval his eyes flickered open. He must have recognised Catsfoot, for his entire massive body suddenly convulsed, like the twisting of a great spring. He tried to shout something, but only a faint sound emerged through the gag.

Catsfoot said: "You're going back the way you came, Guthrie, and I'll be riding with you. Mebbe you're wondering why I trailed you here? I'll tell you about that soon—but not yet. Right now, you're going to get on that horse Al's left behind. I've got mine waiting near here ... now get into that saddle!"

Guthrie jerked himself in a sitting position. By sheer brute strength he tried to snap the bonds. His shoulder muscles swelled like apples under his shirt. But it was useless.

"You're wasting energy," Catsfoot told him. "You'd better get on that horse, unless you want to feel a slug inside you!"

It was pure bluff to make that threat. As he uttered the words, Catsfoot knew that he dare not do Guthrie any serious harm, since the pledge was to deliver him unharmed to Cochise.

Awkwardly, Guthrie began to get to his feet. He was on his knees. Then suddenly he froze still. He cocked his head, listening.

But Catsfoot had heard it seconds earlier.

It was a dull, thudding sound. And it was coming directly towards them. There was no mistaking it—that was the noise of running feet. Now twigs could be heard snapping. Foliage swished as it was thrust aside.

Catsfoot remained crouched, making use of the

deeper shadows near the ground. His guns were out and his thumbs rested on the hammers, ready to cock them.

It was Al.

A frantic, half crazed Al burst upon them. He reeled and stumbled to a stop as he made out Catsfoot's dim outline. He clawed at Catsfoot's buckskins with clammy fingers.

In the moonlight his face was contorted, unreal. When he managed to speak, each word came as a separate agony.

"The outfit's comin'!" he panted. "They wanta find Guthrie! I nearly walked into 'em... they're all around!"

Catsfoot stood up. He knew immediately why this had happened. He had seen one of the outfit wake up as Guthrie was about to leave the camp. That man must have stirred the others. And all of them must have decided to see for themselves what Guthrie did to Al....

The risk of this happening had been at the back of Catsfoot's mind. But he had counted on the outfit obeying Guthrie's order to remain where they were. Now it seemed that the temptation to gloat over the end of Al had been too much for them. They all wanted to be there.

Now Catsfoot heard voices. They were faint, but that was deceptive. In a heavily wooded area all sounds were closer than they seemed.

What chance remained of getting away on the

horses? Practically none. The outfit would be sure to hear them and surround them, for men on foot could move more quickly than men on horses amid those thick and dark trees.

The only possible plan was to lie low—and hope.

Catsfoot's eyes probed the gloom. He saw what he wanted. A few yards away a large dead branch had fallen from a cottonwood. There were no leaves on it. But the twigs were thick and they formed a semi-circle against the trunk of another tree. Behind them, there would be little risk of being seen.

Catsfoot pointed and whispered to Al: "Get behind that and keep quiet!"

Al did not understand. He was quivering along the whole length of his body. He was a human jelly. His hands were still clawing feebly.

"They're comin' … they'll kill me!" he whimpered.

Catsfoot pushed a gun hard into the centre of Al's chest.

"*I'll* fix you, if you don't do like I say! Get behind that branch."

The gun had the intended shock effect. Al gaped at it. Then he obeyed.

Now for Guthrie….

Guthrie had not moved from his kneeling position. He was staring in the direction of the voices. Catsfoot put away his guns. Approaching from behind, he put his hands under Guthrie's armpits and pulled.

As Guthrie came over backwards he kicked. Then he twisted his body like a huge snake as Catsfoot dragged him through and over the mass of dead wood. Within seconds Catsfoot had Guthrie under cover.

But the problem of keeping Guthrie hidden was not over—it had scarcely begun.

Guthrie swung his legs round so that they crashed into the wood, snapping dry stalks and shifting part of the main branch. Noise to attract attention was what he was trying to create and he was succeeding. Catsfoot flung himself across Guthrie's ankles, pinning them down and together.

But Guthrie turned his head and the upper half of his body. He was deliberately scraping his face against the rough ground.

Catsfoot hissed to Al: "He's trying to work the gag out—sit on his chest!"

Al did not move. He was on one knee and as far from Catsfoot and Guthrie as possible.

"Al ... you do like I say, or he'll have that gag out!"

He must have heard. But he gave no sign of having done so. Al had become transfixed. He was listening to the outfit.

The outfit were very close. Not more than twenty yards. Their voices came clearly.

One of them was saying: "Guthrie must have found him by now."

And another said: "Sure he must. He wouldn't have let a runt like Al get away."

"How say we yell out for him? We wanta find him before he fixes Al…. I wanta see the look on Al's face."

"Okay, we'll do that…."

They talked some more. Then there was a pause, as if they were all drawing in a long breath. Suddenly the woods echoed as more than a score of voices shouted Guthrie's name. The noise was almost deafening.

It was then that Al moved. He hurled himself at Catsfoot. And at the same time he screamed: "Guthrie's here! I wanta help him … come quick …!"

CHAPTER EIGHT

BATTLE AT DAWN

Two things took Catsfoot by surprise....

One of them was the hideous extent of Al's trickery. He had taken part in a plan to capture Guthrie when it had seemed safe to do so. But now that all appeared lost, he was making a frantic attempt to ingratiate himself with Guthrie by betraying Catsfoot. That was something which Catsfoot could not have foreseen.

Neither could he have foreseen the physical change which came over Al. At one moment Al was a quaking apology for a man. In the next he had become a fighting tornado in his frantic efforts to help Guthrie.

Al landed on Catsfoot's back, hands seeking his throat. Catsfoot, lying across Guthrie's legs, felt a jab of pain travel along his spine. Then sweating fingers pressed against his windpipe. He felt a tightness in his chest as it became impossible to breathe.

And all the time Al was screaming, "*Guthrie's here ...!*"

Catsfoot groped. He located the two smallest and weakest fingers of Al's hands. He jerked them outwards and the grip round the throat was instantly broken.

But Al twisted like a whip and Catsfoot felt his gun belt shift. Al was reaching for one of the Colts, trying to lift it from its holster. There was only one answer to that—Catsfoot went into a fast body roll. The gun was whisked from Al's hand before he could get a proper grip on it.

That roll had saved the gun. But it had also taken Catsfoot off Guthrie's legs. Now Guthrie could move more easily and despite his bound arms he could do a lot.

Guthrie raised his left boot. He raised it very high. In the first weak light of dawn Catsfoot saw the spurred heel....

Guthrie was bringing that spurred heel down vertically towards the middle of Catsfoot's stomach. The sharp, two-inch length of slender steel could stab like a knife. There was no time to jerk out of the way of it.

It was Al who saved Catsfoot.

At that same moment Al threw himself once more at Catsfoot's prone body. He landed full length on it. And the spur sank into Al's back.

Al shrieked like a tortured animal and the shriek was renewed as Guthrie wrenched the boot and spur free.

Catsfoot threw Al off. He rolled again, to get clear of Guthrie's threshing feet. He stopped when he hit the thick trunk of the tree.

There he sprang upright, guns jumping into his hands, the hammers clicking back.

He was barely in time. The outfit had arrived.

They were gathered in a wide and glowering circle round the tree. Some were kneeling among the foliage, some were standing. All of them had guns levelled. All except one....

The exception was a half-breed Indian. He was a small man and in the gathering light his face showed like a maddened cougar, mouth pulled back and teeth glinting. He was holding a heavy-hilted throwing knife between forefinger and thumb. He shouted something in his patois. Then he jerked his wrist.

The blade flew towards Catsfoot.

It was pinning and it made a high-pitched sighing sound, as though mourning its victim. There was a swift and evil certainty about its progress—as if no earthly power could prevent it penetrating Catsfoot's throat.

Then it disintegrated. It shivered in mid-flight and splattered into pieces. At the same time there was a crash from Catsfoot's left gun.

The outfit stared at where the knife had been. Then they stared at Catsfoot. From some of them there was a mumble of astonishment. Then their fingers tightened on their triggers. They were ready and anxious to cut Catsfoot down under a scything of lead. Yet they hesitated, awaiting an order from Guthrie.

One of the outfit was bending over Guthrie, slashing with a skinning knife at the linen bonds. They fell apart and Guthrie snatched away the gag.

He jumped to his feet and he rubbed his wrists. Then he backed away from Catsfoot, watching him through slit eyelids. He backed through the scrub and between two trees until he was concealed from Catsfoot's guns.

It was then that Guthrie gave his order.

He shouted: "What are you waitin' for? Okay, let him have ..."

There was a muffled crash of fire.

It was a crash from many types of weapon— from aged Lefauchez pinfire revolvers, from Winchester and Spencer carbines, from .34 five-shot Patersons....

But it did not come from the outfit.

It came from a point outside the circle. A point which was almost directly behind where Guthrie was standing, but some distance away.

Catsfoot heard the trembling whine of slugs— but none was close to him. He saw trees gashed white as bullets stripped the bark, saw soil and shrubs cascade into the air, saw two or three of the outfit reel with arm and leg wounds.

That volley had been fired from long range, which saved the outfit from serious casualties. But its shock effect was devastating. After a few moments of horrified paralysis, they acted in-

stinctively. They started to run. They rushed
for cover, as far as possible from the gunfire.

They forgot about Catsfoot. And they forgot
about Guthrie.

Guthrie did not run with the others. Not
immediately. For him, this was an exquisite nightmare and he stared through the trees in terror.

Then Guthrie saw them....

He saw the law posse emerge. Matthew, the
deputy, was leading them. Sam Timberley was
there. So was young Shaun Brent. It was a big
posse. It seemed that every able-bodied man in
Gloryrise was in it. Those men were advancing
slowly, relentlessly.

Guthrie took a couple of backward steps. Then
he turned to follow his outfit. But he got no
farther than that. Catsfoot was standing over him.

"You'll stick around with me," Catsfoot was
saying. "We've got to meet up with Cochise...."

The sun was up when they rode out of the
forest. The posse of almost fifty men rode in two
columns. A glowering Guthrie rode between them.

Shaun, who was next to Catsfoot at the front,
said: "Wouldn't it be better to tie Guthrie to
his horse?"

Catsfoot shook his head.

"A man who's lashed to an animal can't move
so fast and we've got to keep plenty of speed.
Remember—we have to deliver Guthrie to the

Apaches by the middle of the afternoon and that doesn't leave us too much time."

"What d'you think they'll do to him?"

"They won't hurt him. Cochise gave his word on that and I believe him. He's a killer, but in his way he's a man of honour."

Shaun asked incredulously: "But if he's not goin' to harm Guthrie, what *is* he goin' to do?"

"I don't know for certain, but I have a hunch. I guess Guthrie has the same hunch, too."

"What is it?"

"I'd rather not say," Catsfoot replied flatly.

They were moving at a brisk trot—the sort of pace which the horses could keep up for hours without a rest. Two miles ahead a barrier of red rock made a tall and jagged line against the horizon. It was Klimber Tops, which could only be crossed by skirting the edge of a gorge which cut through the centre of it. Wagon trains which occasionally used this route between the Mexican border and Gloryrise had to make a fifteen-mile detour round the rocky range. But the way over the gorge was easy enough for horsemen who had a normal head for heights.

After a while Shaun asked: "Did you find it difficult to trail the outfit?"

"It was easy. I figured they'd head south and twenty men riding fast leave plenty of tracks. But I had a real break when I closed in on them and found Guthrie working on Al. That gave me the chance I needed, but it would have failed if the posse hadn't come along. Say ... what made all these hombres decide to follow me?"

Shaun thought for a few seconds. Then he said: "I told the folks that you wanted to go it alone 'cause there was no time to wait. Then suddenly something seemed to happen in the town without anyone givin' any orders. Inside an hour a big posse was gathered in the main street. It took us a bit of time to pick up your trail—in fact, we never really found it."

"You didn't! Then how did you ...?"

"We found the tracks left by the outfit, same as you did. When we got in the forest just before dawn we were pretty well lost till we heard shoutin'."

"That would be Al," said Catsfoot. "Mebbe I ought to be grateful to him ... I sure would like to know what the outfit are doing right now."

Shaun gave him an anxious glance.

"Does it matter? They didn't look like they wanted to fight in the forest. I guess they're broken up and ridin' hard into Mexico."

"I hope you're right, but a lot of those hombres have a high opinion of Guthrie. Once they've got their nerve back, they won't like the idea of just watching him being taken away by a law posse. They'll see it as a sort of insult to themselves."

Shaun's face clouded as he said: "Y'mean they might try to rescue him?"

"I guess that's about it."

Matthew, who was immediately behind, had been listening. He urged his horse level with Catsfoot's.

"I figure you're worryin' about nothin'," Matthew said. "We outnumber the outfit by two to one. They wouldn't dare try a thing."

Catsfoot smiled at Matthew as he said: "You could be talking sense, but numbers don't always mean a lot. How many of this posse are used to gunfighting?"

"Hardly any, I guess. They're all peaceful folk in the orn'ary way."

"That's what I've been thinking," Catsfoot said. "But the outfit are all professional gun-slingers. They're all top-guns and they're smart, too. It could be mighty tough if they took *us* by surprise.... "

They were no longer riding in two columns. There was not room. The posse was stretched in a long, single file. Guthrie was in the centre of it. They were on a ledge which ran along the side of the gorge. In places that ledge was a mere four feet wide. At no part was it more than three times that width.

Shaun looked below, to his left. He felt momentarily dizzy as he thought of what would happen should his horse stumble. The drop to the bottom of the rock-strewn gorge was at least three hundred feet. A stream ran through it, looking from this height like a silver ribbon. It was flowing well now, but like many streams and rivers in Arizona, it could dry up in days.

Shaun twisted in his saddle and looked upwards to the other side, where there was nearly two hundred feet of almost sheer rock face. There were a few crevasses in it and some of these were the nesting places of the huge and ugly condors.

There was a feeling of being trapped while moving on a mile-long ledge. Shaun had experienced it when riding out with the posse and now he knew it again.

Yet in the ordinary way there was little danger. The ledge, although uncomfortably narrow in places, was firm and the surface gave horses a good grip. But Shaun could not help recalling that there had been some casualties on the gorge. Those had always occurred when a horse was suddenly scared into rearing by a wheeling condor, throwing its rider into the depth of the chasm. Shaun gripped his saddle pommel firmly with one hand. Timberley was directly in front of him. Then Matthew. Catsfoot was leading by a clear twelve yards.

Shaun decided to keep his eyes fixed on Catsfoot. The sight of that straight and tall back, and of the sun glinting on the long fair hair, gave him confidence. He had the feeling that with Catsfoot there, it was foolish to be afraid. He wondered whether, in such times, Catsfoot gave the same feeling to all decent people. It was almost certain that he did so. It was what Herb Brent had meant when he said that folks would follow Catsfoot. Shaun knew from his reading of history that one man in many millions had the strange spark within him which created a leader. Catsfoot was such a man.

They were approaching a point where the ledge widened, but at the same time took an inward bend.

Shaun watched Catsfoot disappear behind the bulge in the rock face. Soon, in a matter of seconds, he would be following round it and Catsfoot would be in sight again.

There was a double explosion. The sound of two shots being fired at the same time. Then a pause. But the briefest of pauses. The hollow echoes were strengthened by four more shots.

Matthew's stallion whinnied and stood back on its hindlegs. He managed to control it. Wisps of powder smoke were drifting round the bend in the ledge.

Catsfoot reappeared. He was backing his horse, the leathers over a wrist. His "Dragoons" were out and each of them gushed flame for the last time as he got behind the safety of the bend. There he jumped from the saddle and signalled to the whole long file to do the same. Some of them did not understand the order and from farther back there were startled shouts of inquiry.

Shaun raced up to Catsfoot. Matthew and Timberley were already with him. His glistening face was stained with gun smoke and there was a powder burn on a sleeve of his bucksins.

"It's the outfit," Catsfoot was saying. "They've cut ahead of us and they're behind boulders at the far side of the turning. They durned near got me."

Matthew said: "We'll have to rush 'em!"

Catsfoot forced down the ejector lever under the barrel of his right hand "Dragoon." He spun the cylinder, forcing out empty shell cases. Then he reloaded. He repeated the operation with the other gun before replying.

"We can't rush them," he said. "Neither can they rush us. On this narrow ledge it'd be suicide because we could only attack in single file. We'd be picked off like flies."

Timberley said: "It looks like we'll have to go back and make the detour round the side of the rocks."

Catsfoot asked dryly: "How much extra time will that take?"

"Dunno ... six, mebbe seven hours."

Catsfoot looked at the sun and said: "I have around three hours left! Just three hours to de-liver Guthrie to the Apaches. If I don't do that, there won't be a man, woman or kid left alive in Gloryrise by sunset!"

CHAPTER NINE

THE CLIFF FACE

A CHILLED silence settled on the little group at the head of the posse. It was broken by a voice which came to them from behind the bend. The voice of one of the outfit. It resounded against the walls of the gorge.

"Set Guthrie free and we'll let y'carry on," it said. "But if you don't do like we say, you'll spend what's left of y'lives on this ledge!"

Matthew shouted: "We can go back if we have to!"

That was an attempted bluff on Matthew's part. An effort to convince the outfit that time did not matter. But it rebounded.

The voice answered: "You can't go back! Some of our men are at the other end of the gorge, likewise. You're bottled in... unless you hand Guthrie back to us!"

Timberley gave a low whistle.

"I guess that's the real big news!" he muttered. "Even if we did have time to make the detour, we couldn't get out of here."

They all looked at Catsfoot. But he seemed unaware of them. His head was back and he was staring at the gaunt cliff face which towered above them.

Shaun whispered: "There's no gettin' away from it … we'll have to give up Guthrie. If we don't, this whole posse will die!"

Catsfoot was still staring at the cliff as he said: "And what about the folks in Gloryrise, Shaun?"

"I was thinkin' mebbe if we went to Cochise to explain he might call off the attack. He ain't *all* bad. Y'said he had a sense of honour. If y'tell him what happened…."

But Catsfoot was shaking his head. Suddenly he looked down at Shaun and that hardness was in his eyes.

"I might as well save my breath than go to him with a story like that," he said. "Cochise has made a deal and he'll stand by every detail of it. If I don't bring Guthrie to him this very afternoon, he'll wipe Gloryrise off the map and no amount of pleading'll make any difference. You've got to remember that he has some special reason for wanting to meet Guthrie."

Another silence. Shaun looked back at the long line of men standing beside their horses. On that narrow ledge they looked as if they were hanging from the rock face. Word had been passed back and they all now understood what had happened. But they waited patiently, confident in the leadership of Catsfoot….

Matthew voiced the question which was in all their minds.

"What d'you plan to do, Catsfoot?"

Catsfoot said: "We can't go forward, we can't go back—right?"

"That's right enough. It looks like the only way we can move is down—if we fall!"

"How about going up?"

Matthew scratched the stubble on his chin. He looked wide-eyed.

"I guess I must've heard y'wrong. I thought y'said somethin' about goin' up."

"You heard me right."

Shaun blurted: "But we can't get men and horses up two hundred feet of sheer rock!"

"That's true. But mebbe one man could get up—me."

The three of them then stared where Catsfoot had been gazing. The cliff was for the most part perfectly vertical. There were two places where the angle was less acute, but they made no real difference. The rough surface, with its crevasses, gave possible hand and footholds. But they were no more than possibilities. A man might successfully use a few of them, but sooner or later it seemed he would be bound to slip.

Shaun said in a croaking whisper: "You couldn't get up there!"

"I figure I might."

Timberley mopped his brow.

"Just the thought of it makes me sweat," he said. "The idea's plumb crazy. Even suppose you don't slip, what happens when your muscles start to get tired? There ain't no place to rest."

Catsfoot pointed to a crevasse about half way up. It could not be seen properly, because they were directly beneath it. But it was certainly longer and wider than others.

"I guess I might be able to lay on that for a while," Catsfoot said. "I can't be sure, but it looks as if it might do."

Shaun asked: "Just suppose y'do get to the top—what then?"

"I'll be able to shoot down on the outfit. That'll soon move them."

Matthew bit off a chunk of chewing tobacco.

"You ain't doin' it," he said. "It's just about certain death and I don't want to see you nor any man drop into that gorge."

"You're wrong, Matthew. I'm going to do it."

Shaun gripped Catsfoot's arms as he said: "But the outfit might see you goin' up! They'd pick you off!"

"They wouldn't see me, Shaun. That bulge where the cliff turns will hide me from them." Catsfoot looked at Timberley's horse, then at Matthew's. He added: "You've both got a coil of rope on your saddle-horns. I'll need them."

Timberley said: "So you figurin' on fastenin' a line round your waist and us payin' out the end of it. You've slipped up there, Catsfoot. That'd make it safe if you were goin' *down* the rock, but it won't help none if you fall when you're goin' up."

"I wasn't thinking that way," Catsfoot said. "I just want you to knot those two coils together for me. If I'm lucky, you'll see what I want them for later."

Shaun said: "Nothin' will stop you from doin' this?"

"Nothing, Shaun. And I can't delay any longer. There's not much time."

Timberley had knotted the two ropes. He quickly re-spun them into a single coil, which Catsfoot slung over a shoulder. Then Catsfoot unfastened the leg cords of his holsters, so that they would not restrict his movements. He smiled at Shaun and said: "This is it—and mebbe it'd be better if you don't look … !"

He reached for the nearest cleft in the rock.

At first it was easy—too easy. The crevasses were conveniently placed and he climbed rapidly. It was when he was fifty feet above the ledge that Catsfoot knew he was making a mistake. By moving fast he was putting too great a strain on his hands and arms. Already the muscles were aching. He slowed the rate of climb.

All the time he was pressed flat against the rough rock. He moved in a series of careful jerks. First he groped with one hand for a new finger-hold.

When it was found he placed his other hand in the crack. Then he dragged his legs up until a place to lodge his toes was located. That done, a hand went up again, repeating the sequence.

Sweat was oozing from him. It was particularly thick on his fingers. It was the sweat there which nearly brought disaster. The greasy moisture was partly absorbed by sandy rock dust and it formed into a thin paste. A slippery paste....

Catsfoot found what seemed to be a good hand-hold. He was drawing his legs up. And his fingers started to slide out of the crevasse.

In a moment of distilled horror he knew why.

And he knew that there was only one chance. Somehow he must wipe the sweat-and-dust paste away.

He rammed his left hand as far as it would go into the crevasse, although that was only two or three inches. Then he whipped his other away. He rubbed it frantically against his buckskins. That dried it, made it less slippery.

But meantime his whole weight was being held by a single hand—a hand which had again almost slipped out of the crack. He made a transfer with only a second to spare.

With both hands comparatively dry, he was able to get a firm grip. But the extra strain had been as much as his muscles could take. The pain had become an agony and the flesh was throbbing.

Somehow he found a toe-hold and that helped a little. But for long seconds he could not move. All he could do was cling like a fly.

He glanced down. Far, far below he saw faces staring up from the ledge. The faces of tense, anxious men who dared not even call a word of encouragement in case it should disturb his concentration. And farther down still, at a sickening depth, was the bottom of the gorge. It looked narrow and dark. Yet strangely inviting. As if saying to him: "*Why struggle? It's no use. Let go and you will feel nothing ... it will all be over so soon....*"

Catsfoot had to struggle to drag his eyes away from the ghastly temptation. But he did so. And he stared directly up.

Not ten feet above his head was the big crevasse.

He could see it clearly. It was very large, as he had thought when he had first examined it from the ledge. It was long enough and wide enough for a man to stretch full length on it. There he could rest before making the last part of the climb—if he could reach it.

Catsfoot knew that he dare not delay any longer. Now his whole body was quivering under the strain. But his brain was once more on ice. It had to be. A miscalculation of a fraction of an inch and he would drop hundreds of feet.

He reached, groped, and found a new finger-hold. Slowly—very slowly—he pulled himself up.

Next he found a knob-like piece of rock. It gave a firm grip.

And now his left hand clutched the edge of the big crevasse. The other joined it. His eyes were shut as he raised himself and rolled on to the platform set in the cliff face. And there he sprawled, all but helpless with exhaustion.

Shaun whispered: "He'll be able to rest awhile now! He'll be okay!"

But Matthew suddenly pointed and shouted: "Look! Look what's happenin' to him...!"

Catsfoot heard a sound like the chattering of a witch. It was harsh and evil.

At first he listened to it without opening his eyes. Without sensing danger. But the noise became louder. There was unmistakable menace in it. Then Catsfoot saw it. Saw the condor. The huge, black-plumed bird was hovering over him, only an arm's stretch away, its wings spreading fully ten feet, its eyes wicked in its loathsome pink head.

It dived on Catsfoot. Dived for his face, hooked beak forward like a warped spear. Catsfoot pushed out his hands. They brushed against long, rough feathers. He felt the formidable weight of the vulture's body. He smelt the stink of its breath, made rotten with decaying flesh.

Then, in a new crescendo of squawking, it was

The condor dived savagely for Catsfoot's face.

gone. It was wheeling wide over the gorge. And Catsfoot saw why it had attacked. Why it would surely attack again. At one end of the crevasse, just beyond his feet, there was a large and crude nest. Condors would relentlessly attack anyone or anything which came near their nesting places— even, it was said, the jaguars.

Now the bird was completing its circle over the gorge. It was returning. It would have to be killed. It would be certain death to attempt to resume the climb with the condor there.

Catsfoot drew his guns. He tried to level them. Tried to take aim. But he could not do so.

It was an easy target for a top-gun. But Catsfoot could not draw a bead on it. His guns were shaking. He could not hold them steady. Those arm muscles were the reason. They were still strained, still quivering.

The condor again checked its flight when it was close to Catsfoot. It rose almost vertically, ready for the drop attack. Catsfoot rammed one gun back in its holster and used the free hand to steady his right wrist. It made no difference. The barrel was waving wildly. It was worse than ever.

Suddenly something was happening to that condor. It shuddered. Then it turned on its side and made three feeble movements with a single wing. And with a final fading squawk it dropped. Dropped like a stone into the gorge.

At the same time the sound of a shot was reverberating. It was the crack of a Winchester.

Catsfoot looked down.

On that ledge Matthew was waving to him and holding a carbine aloft. It was Matthew who had saved him. He waved back. Then he rested. But at the same time he rubbed his arms and quickly the fatigue in them passed away. After ten minutes Catsfoot stood and braced himself to continue the climb.

As he looked up he felt his confidence fade. It was still nearly a hundred feet to the top and the sheer rock seemed invincible. To tackle it was like accepting an invitation to disaster.

Then he noticed that from here on the cracks were more frequent and much deeper. That was probably because there was more weather erosion nearer the top. But whatever the reason, they would give easy hand and foot-holds.

Carefully, Catsfoot memorised the positions of the best crevasses. And he climbed again, with new hope.

That hope was justified. He was weary when at last he hauled himself over the top and reached a wilderness of cacti and boulders. His limbs were aching once more, but he was scarcely aware of that. He knew only that he had succeeded in the vital and most dangerous part of his plan. He paused for only a few moments to recapture his breath. Then, with his long and silent steps, he moved between the rocks. He moved like a wraith until he judged he was directly over the place where the outfit had placed themselves.

Lying flat, he stared down. And he saw them. About a dozen of the outfit were sprawled behind large stones on the ledge. Some, with rifles, seemed to be keeping watch on the bend. But most were talking and three looked as if they were playing cards.

Catsfoot prepared himself methodically. First, he re-knotted the holster leg-cords. Then he pulled out his guns and examined them for any sign of damage which might have occurred during the climb. He could find none. The cylinders were revolving sweetly and there were no marks on the barrels.

He tested the guns for steadiness. They still shook—but not much. In any case, that no longer mattered for he could rest his hands on the edge of the cliff.

He thumbed back the hammers. And he fired.

The four shots were deliberate misses. They hit the ledge only a few feet from where the nearest of the outfit was sprawled, then ricocheted into the gorge. It would have been easy for Catsfoot to have picked the men off, but he could not bring himself to do so, for they could not defend themselves. He decided only to aim directly at them if they should refuse to move.

They did not refuse. There was a tumult of

incredulous voices. They gazed upwards. And as they gazed they realised that the angle made effective counter-fire impossible. They could scarcely see the man who was shooting at them. That decided them—they ran for their horses. They did not panic, for had they done that and had the animals become excited, some might have been knocked over the ledge. But neither did they waste any time. Within seconds they were riding as fast as they safely could out of the gorge.

And only their scattered pack of playing cards remained.

Catsfoot cupped his hands against his mouth and shouted: "It's okay now ... you can come through!"

He saw Matthew, Timberley and Shaun appear first round the bulge of the rock, cautiously leading the horses. They halted directly beneath him, forcing the rest of the posse to come to an unwilling stop.

Shaun's voice came thinly up to Catsfoot, asking: "Are you hurt?"

"I'm not hurt and I'm not waiting here," Catsfoot called back. "I'll be right with you...."

He took the coil of rope from his shoulder and twisted a running noose on to the one end. He dropped the noose over one of the smaller boulders and pulled hard. Then he threw the rest of the rope over the edge and watched it fall. It reached the bottom with a few feet to spare.

Shaun and Matthew took hold of it, keeping it steady. Catsfoot slid rapidly down it, controlling his speed with his feet.

When he reached the ledge, they crowded round him with words of relief and thanks. But he brushed them aside and went to his horse.

"I figure we've only got a couple of hours to deliver Guthrie to Cochise," he said, swinging into the saddle.

The rest of them had temporarily forgotten Guthrie.

Shaun asked: "Do you think we can make it? There's around thirty miles of rough country to cover."

"We'll have to make it," Catsfoot said. "If we don't... well, you know what'll happen to Glory-rise. It'll be..."

He did not finish the sentence.

Guthrie interrupted him.

"You can meet up with Cochise if y'want to," Guthrie was saying, "but I won't be with you. I'm leavin' you folks and you can't do nothin' about it!"

Guthrie was still in the saddle. But now he had a gun in his hand.

CHAPTER TEN

BID FOR FREEDOM

A GUN in his hand....

And one of the posse was staring in bewilderment and fury at his empty holster.

It was easy to understand what had happened. Guthrie had taken advantage of the time when everyone's attention was fastened on Catsfoot. He had used his speed to lift the gun out of the man's holster.

Now Guthrie's lips were stretched in his parody of a smile. He went on: "I'm ridin' out of here. And I'll ride alone. No one's goin' to stop me. I'll put a slug into any man who feels like tryin'!"

Matthew shouted: "You're crazy! You can't get away as easy as that!"

"Can't I? I figure I can. I'm in a durned strong position. You can't use your guns on me 'cause you hope to hand me over to the Apaches alive. But I can use this gun on any of you. Get it?"

They got it. Guthrie's life and safety were vital if Gloryrise was to be saved. He was exploiting that fact. He had made a master move.

Catsfoot dismounted and took a step towards him. Then he stopped.

Guthrie was saying: "I've been lookin' for a good chance to kill you off, Catsfoot. This could be it. It'll be better if you don't try to come any nearer."

It would be suicide to ignore the warning. Guthrie would not hesitate to squeeze the trigger.

Catsfoot looked past Guthrie—hoping to see some of the posse in a position to attack from the rear. But none could do so. In the excitement of the past few minutes they had all moved in front of Guthrie.

Guthrie pulled hard on the bit and his horse, its eyes rolling with fright, moved slowly backwards along the ledge.

Timberley said something under his breath. Then he snapped: "We can't just stand here and let him get away! I'm goin' to shoot...."

His hand went for his gun. But Catsfoot gripped his wrist and held it firm.

"We're not shooting," he said. "You know why."

"But if he's goin' to escape, we might as well fix him!"

"He hasn't escaped yet and while he's alive there's still a chance of delivering him to Cochise."

Timberley shrugged.

"Okay—but I don't like it."

Now Guthrie had backed his horse to the bulge in the rock face. He had put a clear twenty yards between himself and the nearest of the posse.

He said: "If you've got any ideas about followin' me, forget them. If any hombre comes in range of this gun it'll be too bad."

He turned the horse and vanished round the bend in the ledge.

There were moments of dismal silence among the posse. Shaun broke them when he turned to Catsfoot.

"Isn't there anything we can do?"

"I guess so and I'm going to do it—but this'll be a one-man mission. All the rest of you'll have to stay here."

"What are you aimin' to do, Catsfoot?"

"I'll tell you when I've done it, Shaun. That's if I'm able to do it. Now I want all of you to remember something important—if you hear shooting, don't try to come round and help me. Remain right here."

Matthew gave a puzzled grimace.

"I don't understand any of this."

But Catsfoot was already remounting. At a slow canter, he followed Guthrie along the ledge.

About a hundred paces divided them. Guthrie turned in the saddle when he heard the sound of approaching hooves. Then he reined in his horse and shouted: "You come much nearer and it will be all over for you!"

"I'm coming a lot nearer, Guthrie! I'm coming

right up to you and I'm going to take that gun away from you."

"You talk like there's somethin' wrong in your head! No man can take a gun from me and right now, you can't even try. You can't shoot. You're helpless—so don't kid me none."

"There's no kidding," Catsfoot called back. "Watch me, Guthrie! I'm moving in on you."

He touched spurs. His horse again moved forward.

Guthrie pulled his animal round till it was facing the oncoming Catsfoot. With deliberate slowness, he levelled his gun. He aimed it at the centre of Catsfoot's chest.

But that was no more than a gesture and both men knew it. The range was now about eighty paces—impossibly long for any revolver. Because of their violent recoil, most Colt models could only be used with accuracy over distances of under thirty paces.

So Guthrie waited. He waited with the gun held rock steady.

And Catsfoot drew closer. He sat bolt upright, as though deliberately exposing himself to Guthrie, both hands on the reins. Within seconds the distance had closed to sixty paces.

Fifty, forty....

There was a slight cleft in the rock face just in front of Catsfoot. And Catsfoot's eyes were on that cleft.

He waited till he was level with it. Then it happened. Then he became a human spring. His entire tall, slender body seemed to react as though suddenly released from intolerable tension. He jerked out of the saddle. He flew twisting through the air.

Guthrie was slightly out of range. But he chanced a shot. It was a good one—Catsfoot felt the air movement as the slug passed within an inch of his face.

But now Catsfoot was landing in the rock cleft. That cleft was only a shallow piece of erosion, a mere foot deep and oval shaped. It was as if a giant finger had scooped a piece out of the wall. Catsfoot landed on his haunches within the cover of it. He seemed to lose balance and for a moment he reeled forward, his head becoming visible to Guthrie.

Guthrie tried again. A piece of lead skidded between Catsfoot's saddle boots and shattered against the rock.

Catsfoot pulled back. Standing upright, he pressed into the cleft. His fists were clenched in front of him, as if fighting to resist a temptation to draw his own guns. His mouth was taut under nerve strain.

Guthrie hesitated. Then he got out of the saddle. Very cautiously he walked towards the cleft. After a dozen paces, he stopped and moved towards the extreme side of the ledge, seeking an angle from which he might be able to see Catsfoot.

He shouted: "This time you've not been a whole lot too smart, Catsfoot! I'm goin' to fix you. You can't stay there for ever, so I guess I can afford to wait till you show yourself."

There was a short silence. Then Catsfoot's voice came back. It was a changed voice. It was laden with sudden fury.

"You won't have to wait long, Guthrie! I'm coming out right now. I'll be safe enough because the range is too much for you! Mebbe you draw fast, but you don't shoot so good!"

Guthrie's slab-like face reddened under its heavy tan.

"So I don't shoot so good! Okay—come out and try me!"

"That's what I'm going to do, but I've got news for you. I guess there's no chance of getting you alive, so I'm going to use my guns."

Guthrie's massive body became rigid. For a moment he appeared less sure of himself. Then he shrugged.

"Okay—if that's the way y'want it...."

Suddenly Catsfoot emerged from the cover of the cleft. But only for a fraction of a second. There was a flash of flame from his right hand gun. At the same instant there was a double crash from Guthrie's Colt.

Catsfoot's bullet hit the rock ledge a clear seven yards from where Guthrie was standing.

And Guthrie. The two slugs from his gun were close—very close. They sliced through the loose sleeves of Catsfoot's buckskins without touching the flesh.

The reverberations died away and from somewhere nearby a coyote howled a protest.

And Guthrie laughed. It was a laugh of sheer exultation, of absolute animal delight.

"It looks like I handle a gun a whole lot better than you, eh Catsfoot? I figure this is goin' to be easy! Like to try the same again?"

Catsfoot's voice was shaking as he answered. He spoke as if he were suddenly scared, but fighting to disguise the fact.

"I figure I'll do a whole lot better the next time. You shoot good, Guthrie. You shoot better than I'd thought and mebbe I can't face up to you, but I ain't runnin' away."

Guthrie cocked the hammer of his gun. He was confident. Almost delighted.

"Okay, Catsfoot! You show y'self again…."

Catsfoot showed himself. He did so for much longer than before. For a full three seconds his whole body was visible.

And in that time Guthrie fired twice.

The first of the long range shots was inches wide of Catsfoot's right shoulder. The second—and it followed almost simultaneously—made a pink scar across his cheek. Blood trickled from it. But not much. It was the slightest of surface wounds.

As the echoes died there was one more long silence. A silence in which only the howl of that distant coyote could be heard.

Then Catsfoot emerged from the cleft. He emerged slowly, deliberately. And he stood within full view of Guthrie. His guns were back in their holsters. His hands were relaxed and hanging at his sides.

Catsfoot called across the intervening distance: "Would you like to shoot again, Guthrie!"

Guthrie looked down at his empty gun. He spun the cylinder. Then he groped for his gun belt. A gun belt that was not there. A gun belt which had been taken from him.

With long and silent steps Catsfoot approached him.

"You'd forgotten something," he told Guthrie.

Guthrie's face was confused as he said : "I guess I did. I forgot I hadn't any spare ammunition. But I ain't finished yet! Mebbe you've duped me into shootin' wild, but you've still gotta take me."

Catsfoot was walking nearer as he said: "That's just what I'm going to do, Guthrie. I'm going to take you with my bare hands! Mebbe the time will come when we will meet with guns and I'll shoot the way I can! But this time, it's just you against me. Just your strength against mine!"

It was then that Guthrie ran.

He ran towards his horse.

But he did not travel far. Catsfoot's long strides overtook him when he was still yards from the animal. He leaned against Guthrie's saddle—a barrier between it and its rider.

"You ain't getting out of here," Catsfoot said softly. "I have a job to do and I'm going to do it—that's to hand you over to Cochise!"

Guthrie quivered over his whole vast frame.

"Cochise will kill me."

"He won't do that. He said he wouldn't and I take his word."

"Then why does he want me?"

"Take a guess! That's all I can do."

"I ain't bein' handed over to any Apache! I'll break you in half if you try to stop me gettin' on that hoss, Catsfoot!"

Catsfoot smiled as he looked at Guthrie's enormous chest and ox-like shoulders.

"Okay, Guthrie, I'm waiting. You try to take me."

Guthrie gathered himself as a steer might prepare for a charge. Then he hurled himself at Catsfoot. His hands were outstretched. The fingers clawed for Catsfoot's throat, seeking a stranglehold. And they found it. As Catsfoot tried to move away he stumbled against a piece of rock. He felt Guthrie's fingers circle his neck. He felt the thumbs press savagely against the windpipe.

Then came the agony of not being able to breathe. And with it was the temptation to panic. But

Catsfoot fought down that temptation as he used the classic counter to the stranglehold.

He groped till he found the little fingers on Guthrie's hands. He pulled them up and Guthrie gave a moan of pain as he was forced to release his grip. At the same time he staggered back.

At that moment there was a massed shout. It came from the posse. They were appearing round the bend in the cliff, riding as fast as safety allowed. Before Catsfoot and Guthrie could close with each other again, the posse was between them.

And Guthrie was again a prisoner.

Shaun clutched Catsfoot's buckskins and asked: "How did you do it? How did you get right up to him without bein' killed?"

Others asked the same question. Catsfoot gave his slow, gentle smile.

"If you're still interested, I'll tell you later," he said. "Right now, we've got a lot of hard riding ahead of us. Mister Guthrie has cost us a lot of valuable time."

CHAPTER ELEVEN

DECISION OF COCHISE

HIS arms were folded over his bare and muscled chest. He stood with his war council.

"I believed the white man would succeed," Cochise said, "for he is a warrior such as I. Yet it seems he will not bring Guthrie to me and I am sorry."

An aged Apache, his face shrivelled like an old nut, shuffled up to Cochise and said: "It is good that lie has not come."

"How?" Cochise asked, staring south.

"For now your braves can bring blood and fire to the town and many scalps will be theirs."

Cochise's lean face was blank as he said: "Will my braves boast of such scalps? Does a dog boast of slaying a flea?"

The old Apache, who could no longer draw blood in battle but liked to see others do it, made a fluttering protest with his scrawny hands.

"Why do you speak thus, Cochise? Is it that you are losing the taste for war?"

"War against the whites is sweet to me, like milk to a child. But it will not be war when my braves sweep upon Gloryrise. It will be massacre of the weak and helpless and that is no task for warriors to enjoy."

The old one gave Cochise a quick and doubting glance.

"Can it be that you think of sparing the place?" he asked.

Cochise shook his head.

"The town will not be spared. I said I would destroy it if Guthrie was not brought to me by this time and my word shall be kept...." He paused, then pointed to a pile of tinder greased with animal fat. "Light it," he said, "and give the signal to attack."

The old Apache blinked with dim eyes at the distant lines of braves. There were many hundreds of them and they were ready mounted on their ponies. He sucked his bare gums in anticipation. Then he stumbled forward to pass on the order.

A voice stopped him. It was the voice of Cochise. "Wait!" he said.

And he gestured to the south. Horsemen were approaching. A long, straggling column of horsemen, moving fast amid billows of dust.

"I think perhaps Catsfoot will be bringing Guthrie to me," Cochise added, and he was smiling.

The hot air was sickly with the smell of horses and the smell of weary men. Some of the posse had dismounted. Others stayed in their saddles.

All watched warily as Catsfoot and Guthrie walked forward to meet Cochise.

Catsfoot halted and looked with relief at the lines of braves.

"You've not harmed Gloryrise," he said.

"The town and all who belong to it are safe." Cochise's eyes were on Guthrie. He added: "Is this the one of whom we spoke together?"

Catsfoot nodded and Guthrie made an uncertain step forward.

"You ain't goin' to harm me, are you?" Guthrie asked urgently. "Catsfoot's told me you gave y'word on that, also!"

"Neither I nor any of my people will harm you."

Guthrie gave a loud grunt of relief and mopped his face on his sleeve. Suddenly he ceased doing that and asked: "Well, what d'you want me here for?"

"I wished to see you, for is it not said that none is so fast as you with a gun?"

Guthrie at first looked surprised. Then he gave a smile of pleasure.

"That sure is true, Cochise. I guess I carry the fastest gun on earth. There ain't no one who's ever licked me to the draw and I've kinda lost count of all them who've tried!"

Cochise nodded slowly.

"It is good to meet a man of such skill," he said. "I have heard much of you. But have not all people heard of you, Apaches as well as whites? Men tremble when they speak your name, as they tremble also when they utter mine."

Now Guthrie was grinning broadly. He spoke in friend-to-friend tones as he said: "I guess you and me have a whole lot in common, Cochise. I can understand you wantin' to meet up with a man like me, and it's my pleasure likewise."

Cochise looked at Guthrie's empty holster.

"But you have no gun?"

"Catsfoot took it from me when the posse grabbed me. I sure would like to have it back—it's a special kind of gun."

Cochise said to Catsfoot: "Return it to him."

Catsfoot walked to his saddle-bag, took out the gun and belt and handed them to Guthrie. Eagerly Guthrie balanced the gun in his hand. Then he spun it, finger through the trigger guard, so that the silver butt edging glistened.

"I feel better now," he said as he turned it neatly into his holster. "I'm kinda naked without this Colt. It's just a part of me...." He hesitated, slab-like face suffused with satisfaction. Then he said: "Say, Cochise, mebbe you'd like to see how I draw this gun, eh? I figure that's what you've been hopin' for."

"Yes, show me," Cochise answered. "Show me this speed of which all have heard."

"I'll show you speed and somethin' else as well,"

Guthrie said. Then turning to Catsfoot, he asked:
"You got a silver dollar?"

Catsfoot did not answer, but he produced a
coin from the breast pocket of his buckskins.

"Toss it up," Guthrie said. "Not high—
I don't want you to make it easy...."

Catsfoot flipped the coin in the air. It had barely
left his hand before Guthrie's gun was out. It
was still travelling upwards when there was a crash
of exploding powder. The coin changed course.
It whisked sideways and fell into the sage.

"I can do better than that," Guthrie told Cochise
as he replaced the Colt. "I sure would like to give
you a proper show of gunplay."

"That is why I had you brought here," Cochise
said without expression.

"Durn it! Well why didn't y'say so at first. I'd
be glad for you to see it all. And say... I've lost
m'outfit. Mebbe I could be useful ridin' with your
Apaches? A gun like mine could help you a lot."

The blankness vanished from Cochise's face. It
was replaced by a look of pure, distilled hatred.

"My people fight that they may live!" he said.
"They do not need the help of white traitors!"

"Say ... no offence, Cochise! I only..."

"Be quiet and hear me! You will now prove
to me that you are indeed the fastest gunfighter
in these our lands!"

"That's just what I am, but how can I prove
it?"

"Draw your gun on Catsfoot!"

There was a sudden strained movement among Apaches and whites. Then utter silence. A silence so complete, it seemed no one was breathing. Guthrie licked his lips. His eyes flicked from side to side, between Catsfoot and Cochise. They were uneasy.

"So that's why you wanted me here," he muttered. "That's the real reason."

At first Cochise did not reply. His arms were still folded across his chest. He was as still as a bronze statue. But eventually he said: "I heard that once Catsfoot gave a challenge to you and you refused. Can it be that you, Guthrie, are afraid?"

"I ain't scared of no man!"

"Can it be that the speed of his guns is greater than yours?"

"That ain't true! It can't be true!"

"Then show me, Guthrie! Show all of us!"

"What happens to me if I do that—if I fix Catsfoot?"

"You will not be touched by any man and you will leave this place in peace."

"I've got your word on that?"

"I have spoken."

"Okay," Guthrie said. "I guess Catsfoot's had it comin' to him for a long while. I'll count twenty paces between us and..."

Catsfoot interrupted. He said gently: "I don't see any need for twenty paces, Guthrie.

Catsfoot turned on his heels, upright and relaxed.

We're nice and close now and that sort of makes it more certain."

Guthrie's round eyes were like those of an angry snake. He nodded.

The Apaches and white who were standing close to the two men fell back from the danger area. All except Cochise. He remained entirely still.

"If that's the way y'want it," Guthrie said to Catsfoot, "It'll be the way you'll get it...."

He started to move. He moved slowly to his left, body crouched forward, hand quivering over his holster.

Catsfoot moved with him. But Catsfoot only turned on his heels and he was upright, relaxed. His gun hands were open, steady, and held forward at waist level.

Each man knew that he could not afford to take the slightest chance. Each knew that, whatever the result, only the barest fragment of time would decide between them.

Then it happened and it was over before the mind could absorb it.

There was a reverberating roar which tortured the air and flashes which were like droppings from the sun.

Guthrie was reeling back. His gun was dropping from nerveless fingers. And an ugly pool of blood was seeping through the material over his right arm.

Catsfoot was re-cocking his "Dragoons." They were still aimed at Guthrie.

Guthrie ceased to reel. He clutched at the wounded arm and gazed in terror at the two Colts in Catsfoot's hands.

He screamed: "Don't kill me...! You've licked me, that's enough! Don't... !"

Catsfoot's guns crashed again.

And Guthrie's holster fell to the ground. It had been sliced from the gun belt by hot lead.

Slowly, Catsfoot walked up to Guthrie. He glanced down at the holster.

"I did hear about you doing the same kind of trick to Herb Brent," he said. "I thought you'd like to know you're not the only man who can do it."

Guthrie's face was slack with fear.

"What ... what yer goin' to do with me?"

"Right now, there's a place waiting for you in Brent's jail. There's no lock to the door, but I guess we can fix that."

Guthrie turned towards Cochise. He put out a pair of shaking and imploring hands.

"Don't let him take me! He'll give me over to the law! Mebbe I'll hang!"

Cochise said quietly: "You will surely hang."

"But that's white justice! You don't like the whites. It's crazy for you to help 'em by lettin' them have me!"

"Would that be aiding the whites?" Cochise asked with mild interest.

Guthrie, seeing a chance, grabbed it feverishly.

"Sure it would! While I'm free and ridin' with an outfit behind me I tie down the law in a whole lot of this territory! That helps you Injuns a lot. It makes things kinda easier for you!" Cochise shook his head.

"In war, I do not seek the help of men such as you," he said. Then to Catsfoot he added: "He is your prisoner. I have kept my word and I have not harmed him."

Guthrie shouted: "But listen to me! I'll make any deal you want, Cochise! I swear I will! I'll go…"

Cochise interrupted. He said: "You speak as a coward, Guthrie. But men will always remember you for one thing."

"Yeah…? What's that?"

"In years to come will men tell of how you boasted of being the fastest gun on earth—but you were defeated by he who is truly the greatest gunfighter of them all."

It was then that utter panic, seized Guthrie. Panic which contained the seeds of disaster.

He turned to flee. But flight was impossible. He ran a mere fifteen yards. Then an Apache seized him and others were closing round him. Guthrie jerked himself free. But now he was off balance. He was stumbling backwards.

He crashed into a brave who was standing close to the pile of tinder.

That brave was holding a smouldering brand, ready to light the fire, had it been needed. The brave reeled and dropped the brand. He dropped it on to the greased tinder. That tinder spluttered into smoke-laden flame.

It was the signal for the hundreds of waiting braves. The signal to massacre every man, woman and child in Gloryrise.

They did not hesitate. As the first puff of smoke rose in the hot air, a scream came from mounted Indians. A distant, trembling and ghastly scream. Their lines wavered for a moment. Then they surged towards the town.

CHAPTER TWELVE

THE ATTACK

THERE are moments when the coolest minds become temporarily paralysed with horror. This was one of them.

Catsfoot....

He was standing several paces from the fire. He stared blankly at the smoke, then at the charging braves.

Cochise....

That Apache chief's jaw had dropped slack. His arms were no longer folded. They hung helplessly at his sides.

Shaun....

He fluttered a hand then gave a groan.

Guthrie....

Among them all, he was the first to recover—for he did not care. Already his brain was calculating, seeking a way to exploit this new situation. Hoping for a means of escape.

Suddenly the paralysis ended.

Catsfoot gripped Cochise's shoulder, fingers digging deep into the brown flesh. There was horror in the eyes of both men.

"Only you can stop them!" Catsfoot shouted.

"Get on your horse Cochise and bring them back!"

But even as he spoke he knew that there was no chance of overtaking the braves. The distance to Gloryrise was short. Their start was long.

Cochise ran for his pony. So did all the others, Apaches and whites. All except Guthrie.

Guthrie was standing completely still, glad to be forgotten.

Those were seconds of near-chaos. Scared horses pranced and whinnied as bits were pulled savagely against their mouths and spurs pressed into their sides. Then, abruptly, it sorted itself out. Led by Cochise and Catsfoot, they went streaming off in hopeless pursuit.

It was Shaun who noticed Guthrie. By sheer chance, as he was following the others, he caught sight of the rigid figure. He came to an immediate decision. He must somehow tackle Guthrie himself. But how? There was one way which would take little time. Shaun used it.

He turned his horse and he galloped it directly at Guthrie, approaching him from one side.

Guthrie saw the danger—but not until it was too late. He turned as the left shoulder of Shaun's horse struck him on the chest. It was no more than a glancing blow. But, because of the weight and speed of the animal, Guthrie was flung back like a stone from a sling.

He hit the ground and bounced off it. As he

landed again, he rolled several times. Then he lay still.

Shaun reined in, dropped out of the saddle. Cautiously, he bent over Guthrie. There was a shallow gash in Guthrie's forehead.

Shaun put a hand over the man's heart. It was beating normally. Guthrie had been knocked completely unconscious, but he might recover at any moment.

Quickly, Shaun took off his neckcloth and used it to lash Guthrie's hands behind his back.

It was as Shaun was tying the last knot that Guthrie moaned. And his eyes flickered open. For a few seconds they were glazed and bewildered. Then realisation rushed back to them. He jerked himself to a sitting position, straining against the bonds.

Instinctively, Shaun jerked back from him.

"You won't get away, Guthrie," he said. "So you can save your strength."

Guthrie gave a bellow of fury. Sweat was mingling with blood on his forehead.

"Y'can untie me! If you don't, by tarnation I'll crush you into small pieces!"

But Shaun was already moving towards his horse. He paused with a foot in the stirrup and said quietly: "You'll stay here till Catsfoot comes back for you."

Guthrie began to wheedle.

"Listen kid, I kinda like you. I ain't never

done you no harm. How about givin' me the big break and lettin' me…"

But Shaun was already galloping away, after the others to the town which seemed to be doomed.

A copper miner spurred his horse into Gloryrise. He waved a desperate hand and screamed as he entered the main street.

"The Apaches are comin'!"

He flung himself from the saddle.

"I've seen 'em! Hundreds of 'em! They'll be here in a couple of minutes!"

The word flashed through the town. The people rushed into the street. And in scared voices they whispered to each other.

"Catsfoot's failed…!"

"He never did have any chance…!"

"This sure is the finish for us…!"

But suddenly the moment of fear passed. The people of Gloryrise prepared to fight before they died.

Those people were women, children, and a handful of older men. They returned to their homes. And into their hands a strange assortment of firearms appeared. Some were ancient fowling pieces, others were worn single-shot pistols or cumbersome muzzle-loading rifles. Only a few possessed modern and efficient guns.

Silently now and without fuss they got ready to turn each building into a defence point.

But they would be weak defences. Ridiculously so. They might fire one puny volley. Then they would surely fall to the scalping knives of the Apaches.

Catsfoot and Cochise, ahead of the others, were gaining on the Apaches. But not by much. A gap of three hundred yards was still between them. Across such a distance and over the thunder of hooves no shouted order could be heard.

And the town was a mere mile ahead of the Apaches. It could be seen clearly under the afternoon sun—quiet, serene, utterly helpless.

A single question kept hammering through Catsfoot's mind. How could he attract the attention of the braves?

If only that could be done, the danger would be over. For they would surely recognise Cochise and halt to know what he wanted.

A gun shot might be heard.

Keeping balance with his knees, Catsfoot drew his Colts and aimed them high into the air. He squeezed the triggers. The crash reverberated through his ears.

But it was useless. None of the Apaches looked back. None had heard. To wait until they were within earshot would be fatal, for by then the Apaches would have reached the town.

There was only one other chance. A slender one, calling for all the skills of a top-gun.

Somehow, while at full gallop at a range of three hundred yards, Catsfoot had to drop a slug on one of the leading Apaches. If possible, he had to try to avoid killing the man. Just a slight wound was needed—enough to knock him out of his saddle.

Catsfoot dropped his left gun into its holster. He steadied himself by leaning across the saddle pommel and curling an arm round it. He raised the gun carefully, judging trajectory and allowing for the movements of the horse. At this range, the slug would have to travel in an arc. It would have to fall almost vertically on the leading Apache.

He fired. And he missed. Not one of the Indians fell. All remained intent on reaching Gloryrise for the massacre.

Now Catsfoot took a full thirty seconds before making a new attempt at the nearly impossible.

After squeezing the trigger there were agonising moments in which nothing happened. Then a brave put a hand to a shoulder. He swayed and dropped to the ground.

The others raced past him. But only temporarily. In groups, the long line of Apaches reined in. Startled, they looked at the figure on the ground. That Indian did not seem to be badly hurt, for he was already getting to his feet unaided. And he was pointing backwards.

Pointing towards Cochise, who was now very close to them.

They made a vast gathering round Cochise

while he told them that there was to be no attack on Gloryrise.

Day was not far off, but it was still dark.

Catsfoot finished saddling his horse. He led it from the stable to the main street and knotted the leathers to a hitching-rail. Then he went into the office. He looked through the inner door.

Herb Brent was sleeping on his bunk. And Mrs. Hepple was dozing in a chair, head hanging forward. He smiled, then went up the narrow stairs.

Shaun was lying on his back, the moonlight bathing his face and his eyes tight shut.

Very gently, Catsfoot ruffled Shaun's hair. But not gently enough. Shaun mumbled, stirred, and suddenly he was awake. He jerked upright.

"You're goin', Catsfoot! You're leavin' us!"

"I guess that's right."

"But you can't ... you mustn't. We all want you to stay in Gloryrise."

"In a way I'd like to stay here, too. But I've got my work. I've got the wagon trains to lead and that's mighty important. I figure it's best for me to leave this way, 'cause I don't like a lot of fuss."

Shaun knew it would be useless to argue. There were tears in his eyes as he asked: "Will you come back?"

"I'll be back to see you all. I don't know when, but it'll be sometime. That's a promise."

"While you're away I'm goin' to do something really worthwhile."

Catsfoot sat on the edge of the bunk as he asked: "What will that be?"

"I'm goin' to learn to use a gun—no two guns. Then mebbe the time'll come when I'm almost as fast as you!"

Catsfoot gripped Shaun's wrist. He asked: "Will you do me a big favour?"

"Sure I will. Anything."

"Then forget all about guns."

"But I..."

"Forget them, Shaun. I once told you I wasn't proud of being known as a gunfighter and that still goes. Soon, when you're a man, it won't be necessary for anyone to carry guns any more because the law will be strong enough to look after us. When that time comes Arizona will be a happier territory. And I'll tell you something else—I'll be the first to throw my Colts away when it's safe for a man to do so."

Reluctantly, Shaun nodded.

"I think I understand. I'll forget it."

Catsfoot gave his wrist a final squeeze. Then suddenly and silently he was gone.

In the office again, Catsfoot paused. He fumbled with something on his buckskin jacket, then laid it on the desk. It was his marshal's badge.

He cantered out of Gloryrise as day was breaking.

But at the end of the main street he reined in for a moment and looked back.

He saw a town which was peaceful and secure. It was a town which had tasted tyranny, but was free again.

As he rode away, Catsfoot was happy.